PENGUIN BOOKS INDIA

LABURNUM FOR MY HEAD

TEMSULA AO is a professor at the department of English, and the dean of School of Humanities and Education, North-Eastern Hill University, Shillong. She is the author of eight books, including five books of poetry and a collection of short stories, *These Hills Called Home: Stories from a War Zone*, published by Zubaan–Penguin (2006).

A member of the General Council of the Sahitya Akademi, she was awarded the Padma Shree in 2007.

T0290403

Laburnum for My Head

Stories

TEMSULA AO

PENGUIN BOOKS

An imprint of Penguin Random House

PENGUIN BOOKS

USA | Canada | UK | Ireland | Australia
New Zealand | India | South Africa | China | Singapore

Penguin Books is part of the Penguin Random House group of companies whose
addresses can be found at global.penguinrandomhouse.com

Published by Penguin Random House India Pvt. Ltd
4th Floor, Capital Tower 1, MG Road,
Gurugram 122 002, Haryana, India

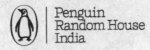

Penguin
Random House
India

First published by Penguin Books India 2009

Copyright © Temsula Ao 2009

'The Letter' first appeared in *The Little Magazine*, vol. VII, issues 3 and 4.
'Death of a Hunter' first appeared in an abridged form in the *IIC Quarterly*,
Monsoon–Winter 2005 as 'Where the Sun Rises When Shadows Fall:
The North-East'.

ISBN 9780143066200

Typeset in Venetian 301BT by Guru Typograph Technology, Delhi

Printed at Manipal Technologies Limited, India

www.penguin.co.in

MIX
Paper from
responsible sources
FSC® C043100

This is a legitimate digitally printed version of the book and therefore might not
have certain extra finishing on the cover.

To all storytellers

Stories live in every heart; some get told, many others remain unheard—stories about individual experiences made universal by imagination; stories that are jokes, and sometimes prayers; and those that are not always a figment of the mind but are, at times, confessions.

Because stories live in every heart, some get told, like the ones on these pages . . .

Contents

Contents

Laburnum for My Head

Every May, something extraordinary happens in the new cemetery
of the sleepy little town. Standing beyond the southernmost corner
of the vast expanse of the old cemetery—dotted with concrete
vanities, both ornate and simple—the humble Indian laburnum
bush erupts in glory, with its blossoms of yellow mellow beauty.
The first time it happened, some years ago, surprised visitors to
the concrete memorials assumed that it was an accident of nature.
But each year as the bush grew taller and the blossoms more
plentiful, the phenomenon stood out as a magnificent incongruity,
in the space where man tries to cling to a make-believe permanence,
wrenched from him by death. His inheritors try to preserve his
presence in concrete structures, erected in his homage, vying to
out-do each other in size and style. This consecrated ground
has thus become choked with the specimens of human conceit.
More recently, photographs of the dead have begun to adorn the
marble and granite headstones.

But nature has a way of upstaging even the hardest rock and
granite edifices fabricated by man. Weeds and obstinate bramble
sprout from every inch of soil uncovered by sand and cement. So
every Easter week, the community comes together to spruce up
headstones and get rid of the intruding natural growth. The
names on individual gravesites are lovingly wiped clean of dust
and bird-shit by loved ones; occasional strangers read them
as incidental pastime.

But the laburnum bush will not or cannot reveal readily who or what lies beneath its drooping branches during its annual show of yellow splendour. That particular spot displays nothing that man has improvised; only nature, who does not possess any script, abides there: she only owns the seasons. And the seasons play out a pantomime of beauty and baldness on the tree standing on the edge of the lifeless opulence, spread over the remains of the assorted dead: rich and poor, young and old, and mourned and un-mourned. The headstones in the old cemetery bear mute testimony to duties performed by willing and unwilling offspring and relatives. The laburnum tree on the other hand is alive and ever unchanging in its seasonal cycles: it is resplendent in May; by summer-end the stalks holding its yellow blossoms turn into brown pods; by winter it begins to look scraggly and shorn. Springtime brings back pale green shoots and by May it is wearing its yellow wreaths again, to out-do all the vainglorious specimens erected in marble and granite.

But the story is running ahead of itself and must be told from the beginning. It all started with a woman named Lentina and her desire to have some laburnum bushes in her garden. She had always admired these yellow flowers for what she thought was their femininity; they were not brazen like the gulmohars with their orange and dark pink blossoms. The way the laburnum flowers hung their heads earthward appealed to her because she attributed humility to the gesture. So she decided to grow a couple of these trees in her own garden which, though not big, could accommodate them if they were planted in the corners, without affecting the growth and health of the other plants. She purchased saplings from a nursery and had them planted at the edge of her boundary wall. She followed the instructions faithfully and hoped that within two years, as the nursery man assured her, the bushes would flower.

That first year, her new gardener pulled out the small saplings along with the weeds growing around them. After loud recriminations, Lentina bought some more saplings and this time, planted three of them in three corners of the garden. She hoped that at least one of them would survive. But it was not to be. One day she heard loud barking and cows mooing very close to her compound. When she came out to investigate, she found that some stray cows on being pursued by her neighbour's dogs and finding her gate slightly ajar, had rushed into her garden and were blissfully munching on the plants they found there, including her precious laburnum saplings. She began to wonder about these accidents in her garden ever since she had planted the laburnum saplings. Nevertheless, she did not give up and the third year too, she planted some more saplings of her favourite flowering tree. Almost miraculously they survived the first few months and began to thrive.

Lentina was thrilled and could not wait to see them bear the magnificent yellow blooms she so admired. But before her wish could come true, another disaster struck. One day, a worker from the health department came while she was out visiting a friend, and sprayed a deadly DDT concoction on the edges of the garden. As ill luck would have it, it rained heavily that night flooding the entire garden. Except the full-grown trees, all her flowers including the laburnums, withered and died. Lentina was devastated and began to think that her efforts at bringing the strange beauty into her garden would never be successful. But whenever she saw these flowers in bloom, on highways and in gardens, the intense yearning to have them closer home began to overpower her. Her husband and children were convinced that she was developing an unhealthy fetish for laburnum and began to talk openly about this in close family gatherings. She could not understand their concern and was inwardly hurt by their seeming insensitivity to beauty around them. But she never gave up her hope of having a full-grown laburnum tree in her garden some day.

Lentina did not mention laburnum to any one any more; nor did she attempt to plant the tree she so ardently admired and wished to have in her garden. Meanwhile, her husband began to show signs of a strange disease and before any proper diagnosis could be made, he passed away quietly one night in his sleep. The funeral services were long and elaborate because the deceased was a respected and prominent member of society. On the burial day, while the hearse was about to leave for the cemetery, Lentina surprised everyone, including herself, by announcing that she was going to accompany her husband on his last journey. Usually it is men who take part in the last rites at the gravesite and stay on to supervise the erection of the temporary fence around the fresh grave. But when Lentina saw the group, including her sons and her own brothers, stepping out of the house behind the hearse, some impulse urged her to join them. Her words were met with silence, because no one was prepared to voice dissent at such a moment. So the party departed, and in the graveyard while the last prayers droned on, Lentina stood among the assortment of headstones and began ruminating on man's puny attempts to defy death; as if erecting these memorials would bring the dead back to life.

Lentina decided that she did not want any such attempt at immortality when her time came, and at that thought she experienced an epiphanic sensation: why not have a laburnum tree planted on her grave, one which would live on over her remains instead of a silly headstone? This way, even her lifelong wish to have such a tree close to her would be fulfilled. In spite of the sombre occasion, she began to smile but when a relative saw her, she quickly went back to looking appropriately bereaved. But the sense of elation she felt could not be hidden for long. So she looked around for her driver and gesturing to him to follow her made her way home.

That night she could not sleep from excitement: it was as if a big problem had solved itself; but how was she going to accomplish it? It was clear that she could not confide in her relatives or children; so she had to find someone who would understand her deep-seated longing for the yellow wonders. She turned her attention to her servants: whom among them could she trust? Not the cook or the gardener, they had families, and secrets in families are never sacrosanct. Suddenly her mind turned to the driver who had been in their employment for more years than she could remember. He was a widower. She decided to make him her confidant. She would take him for a drive the next day to the cemetery and would explain to him what she wanted for a headstone when she died, and why. But there would be one condition: she had to see the tree bloom during her lifetime. The driver's name was Mapu but every one called him Babu because Lentina's grandson called him by that name, unable to pronounce Mapu at first. The name stuck and Mapu good-naturedly did not object even when the older people began calling him Babu.

The next morning, she sent for Babu and they took the road to the cemetery. This in itself would not appear strange: a widow paying a visit to the grave of her husband. But Lentina's intention was different; she wanted to survey the still-empty sites and to reserve a spot where she would be buried. It had to be a spot which would not be disturbed in a long while and would not pose any problem for others. When they reached the cemetery, instead of heading towards her husband's grave, Lentina marched to the extreme corners of the ground, as if looking for a lost treasure.

After what seemed to be an arduous trek, she settled on a spot in the southernmost tip of the cemetery and began to nod her head, as if she had found what she was looking for. Babu was puzzled and was almost beginning to see what his young masters had said about madam losing her mind. When she gestured to him to approach, he went hesitantly. Motioning to him to walk faster, she pointed to the spot where she was standing and said loudly, 'This is my spot, I want to be buried here when my time comes.'

Babu was taken aback and began to protest, 'But madam, your place is already earmarked beside my master!'

'Nonsense, it can go to whichever son goes first. My place is here and you are going to see that the Town Committee gives a written commitment on this. But mind you, no one at home is to be told.' She knew that Babu's son-in-law was a petty officer in that office. 'Arrange it with your son-in-law. I'll pay whatever amount it costs. And also swear him to secrecy just as you are going to do now. Will you keep my secret?'

Babu, seeing the fire and intensity in her eyes, answered, 'Yes madam, I will keep your secret and I will see to it that my son-in-law does the same.' Lentina added, 'He is not to tell even his wife.' Babu nodded and said, 'Yes madam.' Having made this momentous decision, she stretched her hand to him and with her leaning on him, they made their way to the car parked outside the gate and came home. The old woman looked exhausted and went straight to bed. No one thought it strange, because the funeral activities had taken a lot out of everyone and even the young women of the household were looking forward to an early night. But lying in bed, Lentina was wide awake and planning her next move: she wanted to plant a laburnum tree on her gravesite while she was still alive to ensure that all this trouble of securing the plot and keeping everything quiet had the desired results. She *had* to see the tree bloom before she breathed her last. Even for this task she had to enlist the help of her faithful Babu. But unfortunately it was almost winter and they had to wait till the next spring.

In the meantime Babu began the preliminary discussions with his son-in-law about reserving a plot in the cemetery. At first the young man was puzzled; why was his father-in-law talking of such a morbid subject? Was he suffering from some terminal disease that he had kept secret from his own family? But he kept his thoughts to himself. From him Babu learnt that most people wanted the front rows in the cemetery and there was always some dispute or the other about such issues among the more prominent people of the town. Babu's request surprised his son-in-law because it was for the most insignificant plot in the cemetery. He assured his father-in-law that as far as the location went, he could foresee no trouble at all. But, he told him that there had to be an official request; only then could the Committee take appropriate action.

Babu informed his mistress about this and once again Lentina was faced with a dilemma. Should she sign on the application form or devise another ploy to keep the identity of the applicant secret? The latter seemed to be a better idea but how was she going to achieve it? As she pondered, she remembered a conversation she had with her husband long ago. They were discussing the prospects of real estate and he had said, 'If you want to gain from investments in land, go for inconspicuous plots, but ones which have future prospects. That way no one will pay attention when you buy it, and when the town expands, your holdings will appreciate in value many times over.'

Taking a cue from this, she abandoned her original idea of buying a plot in the already-congested cemetery and went for another visit there the next day. This time she invited Babu to walk with her around the perimeter of the wall, and told him to examine the direction in which the cemetery would expand. Babu at once caught on and asking her to rest a while did a quick survey of the surrounding area and came to a conclusion. He helped her to the car and after they were seated comfortably, he said, 'Madam, the land adjoining the southern boundary will be the best, though I do not fully understand why you want to do this when a small plot of land would serve your purpose.' She looked at him with a glint in her eyes and replied, 'Be patient Babu, time will answer your question.' With that enigmatic reply she dismissed him and they drove home in silence.

Once again, Lentina withdrew to her bedroom and began to worry about the prospects of acquiring the adjacent plot of land. The only person she could rely upon to accomplish this was Babu; she decided to entrust him with the job. But before she could talk to him, fate intervened and an opportunity presented itself to her in the person of a man from a neighbouring village who was the son of her late husband's friend. The friend himself was dead and the son, named Khalong, had been away at the time of her husband's death. When he heard about it he came to pay his condolences. Lentina noticed a certain dejection in Khalong's demeanour and when she pressed for a reason he blurted out how bad his financial situation had become as a result of the father's prolonged illness and many hospitalizations outside the state. He sighed, 'If only I could sell our land! But unfortunately now that the cemetery has expanded, people only laugh at me when I talk of selling our land adjoining it. They even joke about it and say, turn it into another cemetery and charge rent! Aunty, I do not know what is going to happen to us.' The poor man was on the verge of tears but Lentina, instead of sympathizing, appeared to become excited about his outburst.

After what he considered to be a period of rude silence, Lentina turned to him and began to ask for the details of his land. Khalong thought that it was simply her way of expressing concern. But what came next completely floored him. 'Will you sell that piece of land to me?' she asked in an excited manner. He could not answer immediately because he was debating with himself whether it would be right to sell her a piece of unsuitable land just because she felt sorry for him. It would amount to taking advantage of her sympathy and would certainly be unethical. Reading his mind correctly, the old woman said, in a gentle voice, 'I know what you are thinking, but let me assure you that it is not merely out of my concern for you that I am doing this. I have a selfish motive. For quite some time now I have been looking for a suitable plot where I want to be buried. And before you say anything, let me add that I do not wish to be buried among the ridiculous stone monuments of the big cemetery. I need a place where there will be nothing but beautiful trees over my grave. So, tell me now, will you sell your land to me?' Khalong was convinced that Lentina meant business and uttered a feeble 'Yes'. But the woman was not done yet; she continued in the same serious tone, 'Listen, I will buy the land only on one condition: you are to tell nobody about the transaction yet, not even your wife. If you agree to this condition, tell me how much you want and come tomorrow with the documents and we will finalize the deal.'

Khalong was so overcome by the unexpected turn of fortune that he stated an amount beyond his expectation. He was even more shocked to hear her say, 'Ok, come tomorrow at eleven.' He did not wait for any formal dismissal after she gave her instructions, hurrying out of the house in a daze, still wondering whether all that had transpired was actually real. Lentina knew that had she bargained a bit, the price would have been reduced but she felt that heaven's gifts should be accepted without any murmur, and simply proceeded to put together the amount needed for the next day's transaction. Once again she enlisted the help of Babu who was to be a witness to the deal. When Babu reminded her about the negotiation with the Town Committee and that he would have to explain the abrupt halt to his son-in-law, Lentina smiled and told him, 'Let him think that it was a wild scheme thought up by someone going senile.'

As instructed by Lentina, Khalong came with the thumb-print of a relative on a paper where the Agreement was inscribed. The deal was accomplished without a hitch and Lentina became the proud owner of a plot of land right next to the south wall of the old cemetery. Lentina ordered Babu to engage some labourers to erect a temporary boundary fence. It was only when the fence was almost complete that her sons came to know about their mother's 'crazy' plan. They remonstrated with her, they sulked at having been left out of the deliberations and even threatened to move out of the compound if their mother treated them like rank outsiders; they were upset that a mere driver had usurped their rightful place in her schemes. But even then, they were not aware of the full extent of her designs for the new cemetery. She tried to pacify them by saying that she did not want to burden them with tasks which she and Babu were perfectly able to handle. The sons kept quiet but the elder daughter-in-law wanted to assert herself and began to accuse Lentina of putting too much trust in a servant and this, she said, amounted to insulting them. Lentina, smarting from the unfairness of the charge, blurted out something which she overheard during her husband's funeral and had decided to keep it a secret. It was an argument between the two daughters-in-law about who was to pay for the funeral expenses. The elder one had said, 'It is not fair that we alone should bear the costs, you and your husband should pay half of it.' To this the younger one had replied, 'How can I say anything? Tell that husband of mine, if you feel like it. But I am not going to give a rupee towards this unnecessary show.' Everyone knew that the younger daughter-in-law had money of her own and that gave her an edge over the other. She continued, 'And if you think that we are going to waste money on some grandiose headstone for the old man, think again. Such pretensions this family has!'

Lentina had kept this knowledge to herself and had resolved that she would never divulge this to any one. But, being goaded into speech by interference from her family on a matter she thought did not directly involve them, she decided to speak out. She addressed the two ladies, 'Why are you all worked up about such a trivial matter? After all, I have not spent anyone else's money. And another thing: you need not worry about any headstone for me. I want none.' The two ladies were completely taken aback; they had assumed that they were alone in the room when the altercation had taken place. The deft and crafty manipulation of her knowledge helped Lentina put an end to all opposition. When the husbands learnt how their mother 'took care' of their wives, they merely chuckled and muttered, 'That's mother for you. Hope you've learnt your lesson.'

News about Lentina's acquisition of the plot of land adjacent to the cemetery soon became public knowledge, and she knew that sooner than later she would be visited by members of the Town Committee and the issue about 'ownership' would be raised, because all such grounds were to be only in the custody of either the church or other religious organizations, with due permission from the Committee. Anticipating their move, she had already drawn up a legal document with the help of her nephew who had just started practising law in the District Court. In the document she had declared that she would donate the piece of land to the Town Committee, and not to the Church, if, and only if, they gave a written undertaking that it would be managed according to her terms:

1. The new plot of land could be dedicated as the new cemetery and would be available to all on fulfilling the condition that only flowering trees and not headstones would be erected on the gravesites.
2. Lentina, as the Donor, should be the first to choose a plot for herself.
3. Plots would be designated by Numbers only and records of names against Plot Numbers would be maintained in the Committee Register.
4. The terms were to be widely publicized and the Town Committee would ensure that they were adhered to strictly.

As expected, the members came one day and were ushered into the big drawing room where they seated themselves with obvious ceremony, stressing their eminent status in society. Lentina greeted them amiably and expressed surprise at their 'official' visit. The Chairman cleared his throat and began first by expressing the Committee's collective sympathy for the bereaved family. Lentina replied in a befitting manner and inquired to what she owed the honoured visit. The Chairman looked at his colleagues and launched into his rehearsed speech about ownership of sacred grounds and what the Town's administrators had to say about it. Gently but firmly, Lentina interrupted him and said, 'Thank you Mr Chairman, I want to assure you that I am aware of your responsibility regarding the matter and I have taken the initiative to seek your cooperation by drawing up this legal document for your consideration. Kindly discuss this with your colleagues and let me know as soon as possible if the terms are acceptable to you.'

The Chairman gave her a sharp look but refrained from saying anything, though it was clear to all that he resented being cut off in the middle of his speech. He turned to an elderly Member and asked, 'What do you say, brother? Shall we discuss this here or take it back with us and discuss it in the office?' The other read the document and said in a voice more authoritative than that of the Chairman, 'We can do it here; it seems the terms are quite simple. I see no harm in accepting them because the town is getting a substantial plot of land, the need for which has long been felt. The kind lady has indeed come to our rescue, she must be congratulated.' After this emphatic endorsement by an important Member, there was no need for further discussion of the terms. Through another Deed drawn up a few days later, the new cemetery with its unusual stipulations came into the possession of the Town Committee. On the day the legal formalities were concluded, this time in the presence of her sons and their wives, Lentina said, almost like an afterthought, 'By the way, can I choose my plot now?' Every one in the room was struck by the ingenuity of this seemingly innocuous request. It was as if she were asking for a candy, and not for a place where she would eventually be buried. The entire transaction was of a somewhat morbid nature but she took the sting out of it by what she added next, 'You see I want to plant something there.' No one could say anything to this and as the visitors departed, the faint voice of the Chairman could be heard, 'After all, she being the Donor, it is only right that she should be given the first choice.'

Lentina and Babu made frequent visits to the new ground. Then one day Babu drove up with the gardener carrying laburnum saplings which he planted on the prepared ground. Lentina discontinued her visits to the cemetery because she was beginning to feel a fatigue that comes after a sustained effort and achieving a long-cherished dream. How that plot of land came into her possession was still a mystery to her when all she had craved for was a spot to be buried where a laburnum tree would bloom every May. Ah, the laburnum tree! Would the saplings survive this time, she speculated? Would they really bloom and would she live long enough to actually see the trees with flower? Before one knew it, another May with laburnum blossoms everywhere had come and gone. A small consolation for the frail woman was that her plants out 'there' were doing fine. Babu, the ever-faithful friend, for this is how she thought of him now, brought news about many things including that of her treasured plants.

Once in a while she would tell Babu that she wanted to see them herself to which he would say, 'Soon madam, but not today.' Her days were now threatening to blur into dusk. Sometimes they would find her roaming in the garden barefoot and without a shawl. That winter Lentina caught a bad cold and fell seriously ill. Every one thought that she would not last the winter. Even her doctor, usually a jolly person, began to show signs of strain after every visit to her room. Only Babu remained calm and steadfast during the crisis. When relatives and close friends were allowed brief visits, it was Babu who stood guard outside the door to see that they did not stay too long. Sometimes Lentina would pretend to be sleeping when noisy and nosy relatives came to visit; Babu then had the perfect excuse to shoo them out quickly. During the day Babu would disappear for some time and when he returned, he would make straight for Lentina's room. He would tiptoe in and she would turn her eyes towards the door and as their eyes met he would give a faint nod and withdraw. This was a message that he had just visited the trees and that they were doing well. This seemed to provide her with the will to live where food and medicines seemed to have failed.

To every one's astonishment, Lentina survived the fierce winter and one clear February morning she rang her bell peremptorily. The maid went in to find her searching for her gown and bedroom slippers. She offered to bring her tea to the room but Lentina ordered her to take her to the drawing room. She sat by the fireside where her tea was brought and she sipped the hot brew as though she were tasting it for the first time. From that day on, she began to move about the house and resume her old routine of supervising the activities in it. When her daughters-in-law visited, she was warm and amiable with them; occasionally she would even give them pieces of jewellery: a ring, ear tops and necklaces. The sons too, sensing a new spirit in their mother, began to ask for her advice on business and family matters, something which had never happened during the father's lifetime. They were pleasantly surprised to find how sharp her mind still was. They also discovered how uncannily like their father she sounded sometimes! There was a visible easing of tension among them and it became apparent that not only Lentina, but the entire family, was heading towards a healing that was more than physical.

That year, the year of Lentina's recovery, something happened in the new cemetery that only Babu saw; he kept the knowledge to himself. Of the two laburnum trees planted on Lentina's plot, one languished and died. But the surviving one had flourished and, wonder of wonders, even produced a tiny sprig bearing a few yellow blossoms. One could not see this from the road because the plant was still small and the flowers sparse. But Babu frequently visited the site and discovered the shy showing one fine May morning. He was tempted to tell Lentina but decided against it because the excitement might have been too much for her. And, if the plant did not develop as hoped for, the disappointment might have a devastating effect on his mistress, weakened by her recent illness. He was both happy and afraid: happy because the long-cherished desire of his mistress to see a laburnum bloom had been fulfilled; afraid, because he instinctively knew that as soon as Lentina laid eyes on the blossoms next May, she would conclude that the right moment to leave the world had arrived. Not that she would do anything drastic like taking her own life, but she would let everything slide and simply bow out of life, with a contented sigh.

But, for all his apprehensions about the future, Babu knew that he could not hold back the force of nature that had accomplished the small miracle of the first showing that May. By next year, the bush would be taller and the flowers more plentiful; it would become visible to all who passed by that lonely road to the new cemetery. He had to tell his mistress about this, but when? He thought about it for many nights and finally decided that the best time would be the next season's flowering and hoped that she would be alive to hear the good news from him. If Lentina now thought of him as her friend, Babu was also beginning to re-assess his relationship with her. Till the time of her husband's death, though she had treated Babu with civility and kindness, she had always maintained a discreet distance as befitting a master–servant relationship. But she gradually broke down the barriers by showing her dependence on him, first by only extracting 'dutiful service'; then imperceptibly as a friend; and finally a confidant. Outwardly, the protocol demanded by their positions was never breached or altered, but it soon became apparent to everybody how much Lentina relied on the old driver for things she wanted done. And surprisingly, this was accepted by her sons and their wives—it relieved them from the onerous duty of being on call for their frail and aged mother. A strong-willed woman and her faithful servant were thus drawn into an unusual bond of common humanity, based on trust and loyalty.

By the time the new year came, Lentina showed signs of fatigue brought on by old age. Her family watched her keenly all through the winter months and she was never left alone. When March came and the weather became warmer, she wanted to be taken out in the car. Her wish was at first just ignored but when she refused to eat unless she was taken out for a ride, the family decided to accede. And so a routine was established: twice a week, weather permitting, Lentina would go out in the car accompanied by her maid. Lentina did not object to this arrangement and came back from these outings a much happier person. She ate well and some colour returned to her pale face. But during these jaunts, she sat quietly, without uttering a word, and even when Babu or the maid commented on something new or strange they had seen in the town, she did not respond. On return, she would head straight to her room and remain there until dinnertime.

And then another May was upon them and every one noticed a visible change in Lentina; she wanted to go out more frequently. But the doctor put his foot down and the twice-a-week routine continued. Seeing her agitation, Babu approached her door one day and sought permission to speak. He assured her that he was keeping a close watch on the plants and that he was confident that they would bloom this season. He still did not tell her about what had happened the previous year. He promised to give her reports on the days she was forced to stay indoors. But during the outings now, the first thing she wanted was to drive by the new cemetery, to see if the laburnum trees were showing signs of producing flowers. She had seen other trees in town with their gorgeous display of cascading yellow flowers. Her disappointment was acute and after a few times, she refused to go out at all.

And then one day, late into the month, on his daily excursion to the cemetery Babu discovered the miracle that they had been praying for: the little laburnum tree was awash with buttery-yellow blossoms! The unflappable driver gave a shout of joy and darted away, heading to his mistress with the wonderful news. On his way, he rehearsed how he was going to break the news to her. He cautioned himself that he should do it gently, so that his dear mistress would not get too excited. When he reached the house, he walked slowly to the lady's room and knocked gently. To his surprise, he heard a sharp command, 'Come in Babu, I've been waiting for you.' He entered and started to speak but she cut him off, 'I know what you are going to tell me; I felt it in my bones.' He saw that Lentina was dressed as if for a grand occasion and standing by her side was the maid, also dressed. The old lady fumbled for her walking stick and said impatiently, 'Let's go, what are you waiting for?'

The bewildered driver and the slightly dazed maid followed the old lady who suddenly seemed to have a spring in her walk, and proceeded on their apparently routine outing. But only Lentina and Babu knew what this phenomenon signified. Once they reached the site, Lentina withdrew into a more sombre mood, as did Babu; only the maid exclaimed at the sight of the luxuriant blossoms on so small a tree. Lentina gazed at the flowers for a long time and sighing deeply, told Babu to drive to the Park, located about four kilometres from the town and was the highest point from where the entire town could be seen. It was a popular picnic spot and was full of people at weekends. When they reached the peak they found that not many people were around because it was a weekday. Choosing a quiet corner, Lentina and the maid sat down to rest. The maid had packed some biscuits and a flask of tea, which the three of them shared. After about half an hour they drove back home. As she entered her room, Lentina turned to her maid and Babu and shook their hands, murmuring, 'Thank you and God bless you.'

Lentina stayed in her room for most of the week. She turned down suggestions of any further outing and busied herself with tidying up her room even refusing help from the maid. On the fifth day of this self-imposed isolation, she called the maid and asked her to help her with her bath and to dress her in her favourite outfit. Having done that, she ordered the maid to bring her some food as she wanted an early dinner. The maid did as she was told and bade her mistress an early goodnight before retiring to her own quarters.

The next morning when she knocked on Lentina's door with the morning tea, there was no answer. She knocked again but only silence greeted her. She entered the room and found Lentina stretched on the bed; she seemed to be sleeping soundly. Putting the tray on the bed-side table, the maid said gently, 'Madam, I've brought tea.' She went and drew the curtains as usual but when she came near the bed, she noticed a certain stiffness in the body and an unusual palour on the old lady's face. Distinctly alarmed, she went out and urgently called the others, the sons, their wives and all the servants. They all came rushing, except Babu, who stood near a post, crying like a baby. They entered the room and the elder son bent closer to determine if his mother was breathing. He straightened up with a sharply drawn breath and shook his head. When the doctor came, he pronounced that Lentina, the mistress of the house, had died in her sleep.

So ends the story of the un-dramatic life of an ordinary woman who cherished one single passionate wish that a humble laburnum tree should bloom once a year on her crown.

And every May, this extraordinary wish is fulfilled when the laburnum tree, planted on her gravesite in the new cemetery of the sleepy little town, bursts forth in all its glory of buttery-yellow splendour. And if you can tear your eyes away from this display and survey the rest of the ground, you will notice that in the entire expanse, there is not a single stone monument. Instead, flowering bushes take root, blooming in their own seasons on the little mounds dotting the landscape. Hibiscus, gardenia, bottle-brush, camellia, oleander and croton bushes of all hues comprise the variety of flowering plants, and at one or two spots you can see some jacaranda trees trying to keep up with the others. A lone banyan and a few ashoka trees standing on the far edges also seem to be doing quite well. And if you observe carefully, you will be amazed to see that in the entire terrain, there is so far, only one laburnum tree bedecked in its seasonal glory, standing tall over all the other plants, flourishing in perfect co-existence, in an environment liberated from all human pretensions to immortality.

So every May, something extraordinary.

Death of a Hunter

The hunting season was on and the hunter was oiling his much-used gun. He was quietly humming a tuneless song, the reason for the suppressed giggles coming from the adjacent shed where his daughter and niece were husking paddy. As the giggles grew louder, he became aware that the girls were laughing at his efforts at singing. So he began to sing even louder and when he faltered at a particularly high note, all three of them burst out in unrestrained guffaws; the girls even let go of the husking pestle, spilling the half-husked paddy on to the mud floor. Almost immediately the chickens hovering outside the shed flocked in, cackling in glee to peck at the fallen grain. When the girls caught their breath, the niece called out, 'Why are you so happy, uncle? Is there a big animal waiting for you?'

The hunter took a deep breath and replied, 'Who knows? Maybe the big boar who has been eating our best paddy these past years will make an appearance soon. I am giving my gun a thorough cleaning so that this time I do not miss his heart.'

For the last five seasons, the hunter called Imchanok had been after this particularly vicious boar which had been devastating the rice paddies of the village and in his field; the animal chose to feast in the areas where he had planted the best variety of rice. When it happened for two consecutive years, his wife suggested that they change the site and accordingly they planted this variety on the western ridge of their vast field. But to no avail;

21

the cussed boar somehow located that very portion to feast on. The animal, sighted by the villagers on several occasions, was reported to be of enormous proportions, had a lumbering gait, and two yellowish tusks curling backwards, almost touching his hump. Not only that, he seemed to have an equally vicious nature. He ate what he could and trampled over a wide area as if to inflict the maximum damage on the paddy. Strangely, Imchanok had so far not even had a fleeting glimpse of this notorious animal, though it was on his paddy that the most damage was done. Many a night during the cold winter he had kept vigil, waiting for the boar to come to his paddy, but it seemed the animal sensed his presence from a distance and went on to other fields. As he thought of the prospect of felling this animal, whom by now he considered to be his enemy, his hands flew up and down the barrel with the greased-cloth, removing the slightest sign of earlier firings. Even the butt of the gun shone with the newly applied coat of varnish. He then stood the gun on the side of the barn and went inside to check the cartridges. He had recently bought a full packet and had lent only two of them to his closest friend, in return for which he had received a whole hind-leg of a sambar which his friend had shot. Having satisfied himself that he was ready for the big encounter, he came out to fetch the sun-warmed gun, took it inside, wrapped it in its special cloth and shoved it into the top of the wooden almirah in his bedroom.

That evening when his wife, Tangchetla, came home from the field, she found him in a very jovial mood holding forth amongst the regular visitors, sitting beside a roaring fire sipping black tea. Gauging their mood she instantly knew that the reason could be nothing less than another sighting of the dreaded boar. This animal had begun to haunt the waking moments of all the menfolk during the harvest season; whose field would be the next site of this marauder's devastation, everyone wondered. This was now the sixth year and with every passing year they were becoming more desperate, as there seemed to be no one, not even a famous hunter like Imchanok, who could rid them of this menace. For Imchanok, it had become a personal contest, between two strong-willed beings.

Imchanok's fame as a skilled hunter had grown over the years. He was a teacher in the village Lower Primary School but that identity had long been eclipsed by that of the hunter. In this capacity he had also received a reward from the government when a rogue elephant had to be shot after it had destroyed several acres of farmland, many homesteads and trampled a number of people to death. There were other hunters in his village and neighbouring ones too, but every single one of them had declined the offer from the government. In fact they had all said that if there was any hunter who could match the cunning of the rogue elephant and kill him, it was Imchanok. So when the offer came to him, it was more in the nature of an order. The Deputy Commissioner sent a Dobhashi with an elephant-shooting rifle and ammunition. They told Imchanok that he could ask for any assistance from the Village Council for the hunt; he was given seven days to accomplish the task.

This was a most extraordinary situation, one for which Imchanok was totally unprepared. It was one thing to choose when, where, and what to hunt but quite another to be faced with the real challenge. Inwardly he began to fume and say to himself, 'What do these sahibs know about the jungle? Do they think that the elephant will be waiting at a convenient place for me to go and shoot him? Don't they know how intelligent these animals are, that they can almost think like human beings? And the area that they can cover when they decide to run?'

But it was an order from the government and he had to comply. Somewhere along the communication process there was even a faint hint of threat: that those who refused to cooperate in this matter might find their hunting licences suspended or even revoked! The other consideration was his reputation as top hunter of the region. Either way, he found himself committed to a hunt that presented itself in such a strange way. So he enlisted the assistance of his most trusted hunting partners and sent them out on a reconnaissance mission to the areas where the rampages had taken place. When they returned with their findings, they held what can be termed as a war council. They debated long into the night and after a few hours' sleep towards the morning, resumed their discussion to give a final shape to their plan. All the members of this group, being skilled trekkers in the jungle, and knowledgeable in the habits of wild animals, chose a spot in the thick valley to set a trap for the big animal. They knew that because of sentries being posted at strategic points around the cultivated areas, the elephant had gone back to foraging in the deep jungle. The spot they chose was one that had not been visited by it yet. It took the seven men most of the day to dig a hole wide and deep enough to hold a full-grown bull elephant. Next, they carefully camouflaged the hole with branches and leaves brought from a different area.

Retreating to their vantage point, they ate cold rice and drank black tea to await the animal's visit. The first night ended but there was no sign of the animal. Towards the evening of the second day, it began to rain and the hunters hurriedly covered their weapons to keep the rain out of the barrels. Besides the official elephant-hunting rifle, three others had carried their double-barrelled guns as additional precaution; there could be other dangerous animals too. But Imchanok was praying that no other animal would appear to upset their carefully-laid-down plan. The second night dragged on; the hunters were wet, hungry and terribly afraid. Only Imchanok seemed unperturbed; he was taking imaginary aims with the gunsight, inwardly wishing that he had had an opportunity to test his aim with this unaccustomed weapon, which was in his hand for the first time. But he had enough confidence in his own skill as a marksman and prayed that there would be no distraction at the crucial moment. As the night progressed, the jungle grew quieter and quieter. Even the watchers became less alert and appeared to be in the grip of that great stillness that only a dark slumbering jungle can induce. Imchanok was fully awake; he sensed the weariness in his companions and let them doze for a few precious moments before nudging the nearest one awake with a gentle kick to his side. As the chain of similar kicks went round, everyone sat up and tried to adjust his vision in the eerie darkness that seemed to have swallowed up the lush green jungle. They waited, each lost in his thoughts. Then came the time in the dying night when you think that day is breaking but cannot see anything except darkness though the daybreak is so clear in your mind. This sensation came first to Imchanok and he silently shifted his body-weight from left to right. The one next to him caught this movement and did the same; then the next and the next until every single man held his position as if freshly energized by this slightest of movements.

The first signal that there was other life in the jungle came from the frantic flutter of a wild fowl perched on a tall tree some distance away. The hunters tensed up in their positions and waited. The ensuing silence somehow depressed them; another day would go unrewarded. Then all at once the jungle echoed with the wild cries of monkeys perched on every conceivable tree; they were truly frightened of something. In the distance the faint swirling of mist could be seen dispersing in the retreating darkness, ushering the break of day. The screeching went on for some time before the hunters realized that there was another sound in the general din. At first it sounded like the yell of bigger monkeys, but when Imchanok listened carefully, he stood up in his place and hissed to the others, 'He is here.' Quietly each hunter went to his assigned position and once again stood still like a statue behind the covers erected earlier. Imchanok had the highest vantage point, and holding his rifle at the ready, he waited there to face this unfamiliar adversary.

The elephant took his own time straying to the appointed area. He seemed completely at ease, breaking a twig here and peeling a bark there as though eager to taste everything that came his way. Several times he stopped in an open space to have a dust bath, but the earth was still moist from the night; he stomped on the earth in mild irritation. He was still quite a way off and except Imchanok, the others were either too scared to look, or were unable to have a clear view of the elephant's morning meanderings. At one stage the elephant seemed to stand still, as if in deep concentration; from the distance Imchanok saw this and became alarmed. Had he by any chance detected some tell-tale signs of their activities? If so, the animal might run away in fright or worse still, might even try to take revenge by charging at the hunters. But as he continued to watch the animal which appeared huge even from this distance, he heard a low growl which grew in volume until the animal expelled his body-waste, delicately side-stepped the lump and proceeded to demolish more bushes and branches on his way. Imchanok had seen elephant dung before in the jungle and he remembered how the huge lumps would emit a foul smell in the early morning sun.

In the brightening light of the morning the elephant looked calm and serene, happily devouring the young plants and tall grass in his vicinity. He appeared to be in no hurry; he even tried lying down once but got up immediately. He flapped his enormous ears and began enjoying a dust bath now that the loose earth had dried up, scooping it up with his trunk and blowing it all over his flanks. From his position, Imchanok watched his antics with growing concern, the distance between him and the animal being beyond the range of his gun. Besides, the trap-hole that they had dug was too far away. When the elephant was shot, they hoped, he would head for the area where the hole was and would be trapped there. Then the final shot could be fired to his skull through the eyes which every hunter knew was the only shot that could kill an elephant. So another waiting game began.

By now it was full daylight and the other hunters too could see the animal from their various vantage points. The initial terror of the unknown was relieved by the spectacle they witnessed. Confident that at that distance they would not be visible to their prey, they began to watch him in silent fascination. But not for long, because the increasing heat of the day was beginning to tell on the elephant's behaviour and he started to blow his trunk in distress. He rushed headlong into the jungle in search of a shady spot and moved towards the clump of bushes carefully arranged near the hole by the hunters earlier. But before entering the spot which seemed to offer some shade, he stood still in his tracks, darting glances in all directions. He was now close enough for

Imchanok to attempt a shot. But the hunter was not sure if the others had already moved to their secondary positions of safety, chosen earlier for just such a moment. The elephant sensed danger and tried to retreat, but his huge body moved sluggishly. The slow turning of his head was all that Imchanok needed. Taking careful aim, he fired twice in rapid succession into what he hoped were his eyes. The first shot caught the animal full face, stunning him. He turned around and that is how the second bullet entered his brain through the ears and lodged there. Imchanok loaded again and fired two more times. At least one of the two bullets must have hit him because the animal seemed to totter.

Imchanok watched in awe and terrified fascination the slow careening of the dying animal as he tried to keep his balance and still move away. But the bullets had surely found their mark because the huge animal toppled over with a last ear-splitting roar from his trunk. He did not fall into the hole as they had planned but was killed anyway. Later, Imcha brushed aside the praises for his shooting skill and claimed that it was only through divine intervention that he was able to fire at the precise moment when he did. A moment earlier or later, and the bullets would have simply glanced off the thick hide, merely enraging the rogue and putting all of them in mortal danger.

When it was considered safe enough to approach the site, all of them stood in a circle and watched from a safe distance as the life-force oozed out of the huge creature, till the last great heave and the eventual stillness of the huge carcass. As he watched this mysterious process, Imchanok happened to look into the unblinking, unseeing eye of his adversary, lying there so helpless, divested of his menacing power for destruction. Was it his imagination? He would wonder forever because he thought he saw tears in those beady eyes and something else: it was as though the dying animal were trying to convey some message to his destroyer which remained frozen in time; this was to haunt Imchanok for a very long time. The experienced hunter had never once in his hunting career thought of the animals that he shot as anything but legitimate bounty. Killing the elephant however was something else. Previously, he, the hunter had been in control all the time and chose what and when to kill; but it was not so with the huge elephant lying dead before them. The prey had been 'allotted' to him. The sense of accomplishment that he used to enjoy after every kill was missing. True, there was no doubt in his mind that killing the elephant was the only way of ensuring safety for innocent villagers and their fields. But why did it have to be *he* who was placed, in this particular instance, at the centre of the eternal contest between man and animal for dominion over the land?

Imchanok the hunter became even more famous after this episode; he was given a cash award and offered a fine gun. He accepted the money which he shared with his hunting partners but refused to accept the gun, saying that he already had a gun and one gun was enough for any hunter. The administrators were puzzled by his refusal but did not press him any further. What they failed to understand was that Imchanok did not want to be obliged to them beyond accepting payment for services rendered. He had resolved in his mind that never again would he undertake any such task, government order or otherwise. If he took the gun from the government, he surmised, he would forfeit his freedom of choice.

Whatever his private thoughts about this incident, Imcha's present worry was the havoc caused by the old boar. The depredation of cultivated fields was a recurrent disaster for the villagers; but not on the scale of this particular animal's savagery. He remembered one harvest season a long time ago when a pack of monkeys used to eat his grain at the half-way hut on the outskirts of the village. Before there were motorable roads, villagers used to shift the harvested paddy to such half-way huts from where the women and even children would carry the grain to the barns in the village. Since the trek from the fields in the valley was steep these half-way houses reduced not only the distance but also spared them the arduous uphill climb. In this manner, transportation of the harvest was made easy for them. But these huts became the favourite foraging spots for the monkeys because they were not afraid of the women and children who were the only ones to be found there. Not only would the animals eat and spoil the grain, they would often try to intimidate them by baring their fangs and shrieking loudly; sometimes they actually attacked the helpless women and children. There was one particularly vicious male in the group which appropriated Imchanok's half-way hut, and it became dangerous for the womenfolk to try to take the grain out when this group was feeding there. When this was reported to him, he devised a plan to shoot the male in order to scare away the other monkeys.

He allowed the monkeys to feel free and unafraid to feed there by stopping his wife and her party from going there for two days. On the third day he went there at the crack of dawn armed with his trusted gun, and hid himself in a corner of the hut. As expected, the group of monkeys led by the cocky male came after daybreak to feast there. After scattering noisily over the mound of paddy they began their daily ritual of not only eating the same but the babies in the group even started throwing the grain at one another in play, so uncannily like human children. Imchanok was distracted by this spectacle for a while. But when he looked at the huge male, he saw that the monkey had become aware of his presence and had begun to call out in distressed tones, trying to herd them out of the hut. At the same time he was feigning attacks on Imchanok who had by now come out of hiding. Since he was not concerned with the other members, Imchanok took careful aim at the leader and pulled the trigger. But the monkey was quick in dodging the bullet which hit him only on his fat flank. Even then he did not yield; he stood there until his entire group had managed to get out of the hut through the single door. Only then did he try to get away. But the injury to his flank was serious and he became immobile on the spot where he had stood to protect his family. When Imchanok took aim once again, the monkey raised his arms as though in surrender or supplication, and slowly covered his eyes even as the hunter released the fatal shot to his heart. With a groan he toppled over on the ground and lay there motionless. After making sure that the animal was truly dead, Imchanok went to the village and sent his nephews to bring the carcass home.

There was much rejoicing in his family; not only because the menace of the monkeys seemed to have been taken care of, but also because there would be plenty of meat for them for many days. The carcass of the monkey was placed in the front courtyard for all to see. It was kept in a sitting position, its head propped up by a bamboo from behind and in this position it looked truly human! One of the nephews, a prankster by disposition, found a hat from somewhere and put it on the animal's head; someone else brought a cigarette and put it in its mouth. The crowning glory of this circus was a pair of goggles and this was ceremoniously placed above its flat nose. The dressing-up being complete, Imchanok was called out of the house, and when he saw the transformed monkey, something burst in him. He advanced to the sitting monkey and began to slap it alternately on each cheek, cursing it all the time. With the first slap, the cigarette fell out of the monkey's mouth; with the next, the pair of goggles, which was sitting precariously anyway. After a few more slaps the monkey toppled over once more, this time with his legs and forepaws all pointing skywards, stiff, in death. The out-stretched arms seemed to parody its dying moments when it had seemed to be supplicating before his executioner. Imchanok advanced to the grimacing animal and shouted, 'So, you wanted to destroy me by stealing my paddy, did you? Look at you now. You scared and bullied my womenfolk; where are yours now? Another male will take them over while I cut you up and feed my people with your flesh.'

The earlier mood of noisy merry-making now gave way to one of astonished silence at the vehemence of Imchanok's railing. This alerted Tangchetla that something was amiss and she too came out of the house. When she saw her husband's face, she quickly grabbed his hand and pulled him into the house. By the time the monkey was skinned, gutted and cut into pieces, some communication must have passed between husband and wife because when a nephew came into the kitchen looking for Tangchetla's biggest pot that had been used on earlier occasions like this, she flatly refused to give it saying, 'You can use the big karhai where the pig-feed is cooked. No utensil from my kitchen will be used for this meat.' The nephew, though surprised by this, was in a hurry to cook the meat; so he had to make do with the karhai. The unusual outburst from Imchanok, and his wife's strange refusal to lend their biggest pot however, could not dampen the spirit of celebration among his friends and relatives.

They continued drinking and eating the meat late into the night. Tangchetla refused to allow any of the meat to be brought into her kitchen and told the eldest nephew to distribute all the remaining meat to relatives and neighbours, adding that it was her husband's instructions.

Imchanok then did a strange thing. He instructed his wife not to pick up any more grain from the hut where the monkey had been killed. She protested saying there were at least twenty to thirty basketfuls, how could they afford to lose so much? But her husband was adamant: he would not contaminate his main barn by bringing in paddy soiled by a pack of monkeys and tainted with the blood of the leader. So the half-way hut was abandoned with all the grain inside, on which birds and animals feasted for many days. Though the site on which the hut stood was most ideal, no other villager ever built another hut there. Within a year or two the hut disintegrated and was swept away by the summer rains. But villagers still identify the spot where it had stood as Imchanok's bend because it was located at a turning of the jungle path.

The passage of years and the exigencies of a hard life in the village dulled this hunter's sporadic qualms about hunting. Though the spectre of the 'supplicating' monkey troubled his mind for quite some time, he went back to his old way of thinking of hunting as a necessary supplement to gathering food for an increasingly large family. And now once again, an extraordinary situation had presented itself in the form of this rampaging boar to challenge Imchanok as a provider for and protector of his family's very existence. Of late he was also beginning to feel his age; he was no longer as fearless or agile in the forests anymore. So he had started taking a younger person, either a nephew or a friend's son, to accompany him on hunting trips. Also, he would spend more time in preparation for such forays into the jungle. As the boar's depredations increased in frequency and scale, Imchanok decided to go first on a reconnaissance trip to the devastated areas which included his own ripened fields. For this trip, he asked his favourite nephew to accompany him and they set out one early winter morning for the rice fields in the valley.

Imchanok decided that they would not take the usual path but take a detour through a more densely forested area. He told his nephew that he was trying out an idea about the haunts of this very cunning animal which had become the bane of all the villagers. They walked in single file, the old hunter leading the way. His experienced eyes detected some disturbances in the shrubbery around but he did not lay too much significance on that and they marched on. The winter sun that day seemed to radiate a lot of heat and as midday approached Imchanok called for a halt and, choosing a shady spot, the two of them sat down for a much-needed rest. They ate their noon meal at leisure and the nephew went to a nearby stream to collect water in a freshly-cut bamboo container. He was gone for quite some time; in the meantime Imchanok dozed off. When he woke up, his nephew was patiently waiting with the water for his uncle. After washing his face and taking a refreshing drink, they resumed their journey.

As they neared a patch of thick forest reputed to be haunted the nephew was visibly scared. His uncle laughed off his apprehension and started to sing a song. Before he could complete a line, they heard a commotion and the young man turned on his heels and ran back the way they had come. The old hunter was rooted to the spot: the spectacle before him was indescribable. He thought it looked like a boar but no earthly boar could be this big or so black. The animal seemed to tower over everything around him, so huge did he appear. But Imchanok knew that if he were to escape, he had to stun or kill the creature with his first shot. With the instinct of the skilled hunter that he was, he aimed at the head and squeezed the trigger more as an act of self-defence than with the intent to kill. Luckily for Imchanok, the bullet seemed to have found its target because the animal took one gigantic leap and plummeted into the dark forest. There was stillness after that. Mindful of the danger of facing a wounded animal, he carefully retreated the way they had come in the morning wondering what had happened to his nephew. As he retraced his steps, he kept looking back, expecting at any moment to see the huge animal charging at him. But each time, he was relieved to see that there was nothing behind him.

The sun was dipping on the horizon and Imchanok was beginning to feel a little cold, from the cooling day as well as from the release of intense tension. At the next bend he found his nephew, huddled on his haunches and shivering. He looked wordlessly at his uncle and managed a sheepish grin. The older man lifted him up and made him walk in front, unlike the order when they had set out from the village. Contrary to their easy banter of the morning, the two now walked on silently all the way to the village. When they reached Imchanok's house, they found a lot of people waiting for their return, wanting to know if they had seen any sign of the beast. Neither of them responded to their queries at first; but eventually Imchanok spoke: 'I think I have shot the boar.' At this the entire group burst into shouts of joy and relief. They began to ask all sorts of questions, to which the hunter only said, 'I have never seen anything like this before in my life and I don't want to have anything to do with it.'

'But you have to show us where you shot it; otherwise how

can we go looking for the carcass?' Imchanok kept quiet and when pressed further, he simply told them, 'Tomorrow is another day and let's wait for what it brings to us.'

The next morning the village sentries brought news that there was no sign of the boar or even the lesser ones in the paddy fields throughout the night. This was interpreted as confirmation of the killing of this menace and the villagers once more requested Imchanok to give them directions so that they could organize the search party to collect the carcass. Being convinced that the boar was indeed dead, he told them the direction that he and his nephew had taken the previous day. The villagers were taken by surprise, and an elder asked, 'But what prompted you to take this route? Didn't you know that it goes directly through the haunted forest?'

Imchanok replied, 'Yes, but something inside me kept urging me to follow that path. And in fact the boar will be found right at the entrance to the forest.' When asked if he too was going to accompany them, Imchanok replied, 'My job is done; I want to rest for a long time.'

So a party of twenty able-bodied young men was formed to go in search of the carcass of the boar and haul it home. Before setting out, they decided that because of its bulk the animal would be slaughtered in such a way as to make four loads, each load to be carried by four men. The rest would then relieve them in turns so that there would always be four men as lookouts. The group, armed with daos, spears and a gun marched out of the village with much joking and laughing in anticipation of the big feast that would take place after their return from the successful search. They reached the general area in pretty good time because the anticipation of bringing home such a prize had put a spring to their gait. They set out in groups of five in different directions.

The men going towards the entry to the forest detected what they thought was dried blood on twigs; a little further off, they discovered a spot where the tall grass was flattened in a peculiar manner. They surmised that the boar had fallen on that spot but beyond this there was no other indication to show where the wounded animal had vanished. Unable to detect any more tell-tale signs, they came back to the designated location to meet with the other parties who were already there with similar stories. Though the countryside was dotted with tantalizing bits of dried blood, there were no other promising leads to launch another foray into the jungle. They returned to the village a dejected lot.

The search for the boar's carcass was carried on for two more days, covering a vast area but with the same result: no sign of that monster, dead or alive, anywhere. In the meantime a strange phenomenon was unfolding: Imchanok, the famed hunter who had never been known to suffer from any serious illness, took to bed complaining of severe headaches. He lay there listless and did not allow any visitors into his room. Even his own children were kept out; the only person who administered to him was his wife. His paddy was harvested by relatives and well-wishers and brought home.

Only Tangchetla knew what went on at night. Imchanok, the fearless hunter, would shriek out in his sleep crying, 'Look at him, he is as big as a barn and as black as charcoal.' Then he would begin to whimper in Tangchetla's arms, 'I am afraid, woman, he is going to come after me.' It took all her cajoling and consoling to coax him into sleep. This strange phenomenon was further complicated by Imchanok's refusal to eat anything. After several nights of this, out of desperation she suggested to him that they should go to the exact spot from where he had fired his gun and ask for forgiveness from the creature so that Imchanok's nightmares would end. At first Imchanok was sceptical and dismissed her advice as 'woman-talk'. But she continued to nag him throughout the day and even threatened to tell his father about his strange dreams. He still hesitated for another week and the nightmares continued. After a particularly trying experience, Imchanok turned to his wife and said, 'Let's do it.'

So the next morning, husband and wife set out from the village, much to the surprise of friends and relatives. The man looked calm and composed with no sign of any illness, either on his face or in his demeanour. The most surprising thing was that for the first time in his life the hunter was without his gun. The couple looked as though they were going out for a stroll. When they were nearing the area, Imchanok became visibly tense but Tangchetla pretended not to notice and choosing a shady spot lay out their mid-day meal on the ground. Imchanok began to eat the simple food with relish and declared that his wife's cooking never tasted as good as this in the house. After finishing his meal, Imchanok told his wife that he was going to the stream for a drink. Not wishing to let him go alone in his present state of mind, she followed him after a short while. When she reached the bank, she saw her husband standing in the stream holding something to his breast. She called out and asked him what he was doing. He did not seem to hear her at first. She called out his name once again and asked him what he had in his hand. This time he turned slowly towards her and held up a boar's tooth, the aged bone washed clean by the stream, shining like ivory. Wordlessly he pointed to a nearby clump of bushes where tufts of black fur lay strewn among what appeared to be the bones of a huge animal. On their way back, Imchanok stood on the very spot from where he had fired the fatal shot and did a strange thing. He tore out a tuft of his hair and blew it towards the haunted forest, and without a backward glance retraced his steps towards the village. Tangchetla followed him, full of awe and wonder at the mystery surrounding the killing of this beast. And that night, for the first time since the boar hunt, Imchanok slept like a baby in his wife's embrace.

Though his nightmares vanished, Imchanok was gripped by the mystery of the bizarre closure of the boar's killing. The couple decided not to say anything about the discovery of the tooth and bones and they resumed their normal activities as if nothing untoward had happened. But Imchanok's mind went back constantly to the day that he had stood in the stream holding the boar's tooth and how, before leaving the forest, some inner urge had compelled him to enact the strange ritual. But the most acute of those recollections was how he had felt a new sensation, as if a new power was surging within him. Outwardly he behaved as if nothing extraordinary had happened; but inwardly he began to question the failure of expert trekkers to locate the carcass of such a big animal which had not strayed far from where he was shot. And why was it left for him, the hunter, to discover the remains?

He pondered over this for many days and inexorably all his earlier qualms after killing the elephant and the monkey returned to haunt him anew. He became listless and morose; some days he would sit by himself and re-live the life of Imchanok the hunter and his earlier sense of pride about his skill and reputation as a famous hunter, would be replaced by shame and regret. Tangchetla noticed this but kept her counsel, taking solace in the fact that Imchanok's gun was securely wrapped in the same bundle since the boar hunt.

One day when he was alone in the house, he took out his gun from its sack, and dismantled it. The next morning, Tangchetla watched as her husband dug a hole in the backyard humming a tuneless song. And in that gaping wound of the earth he buried the boar's tooth, the dismantled gun and Imchanok the hunter.

The Boy Who Sold
an Airfield

No one could say when the young boy became a fixture in the transit camp of American soldiers, stationed in make-shift buildings on the perimeter of the barely functional airfield, after the Great War was over. These soldiers were part of the contingents who had fought in the Indo-Burma sector and were now engaged in the task of facilitating the shipment of odds and ends left over from the war effort, including settling of accounts with all the local contractors and suppliers. The camp was situated in a town called Jorhat in Assam, and the boy must have come from the hills adjoining the state because he did not look like a local boy.

He was a young tribal boy who had run away from his home and had been doing menial jobs in households in the plains of Assam for a number of years.

He was in the third house where he was beginning to show signs of settling down as a domestic servant. His father learnt about his whereabouts after a lapse of eight months and the following winter he came down from the hills and began searching for him. When he eventually located him, the son refused to go back. The father tried to persuade him saying his mother was heart-broken and had become quite ill. Reference to his mother did not make him change his mind. Instead, the boy looked belligerently at his father and said, 'Why don't you beat her up for this too?' The father cringed before the son's retort and without saying another word left the house where his son was working. It was only then that his employer understood why the young boy had left home and village to live the life of a servant in strange households.

The boy, whose name was Pokenmong, was around twelve when he left home and had grown taller in the course of the last three years; he was moving from house to house looking for any kind of work that would buy him two square meals a day. His present employer, a railway lineman named Jiten Das, having realized why Pokenmong had run away from home, began to treat him with more kindness after the father's visit. Once in a while, he would take the boy with him to the railway crossing and sometimes would allow him to wave the green flag when the all-clear was signalled to an approaching train. The boy was thrilled and begged to be taken to the little signal hut more often. Slowly, a new warmth began to grow in their relationship and almost spontaneously Pokenmong started calling Jiten 'Baba'. When he said it the first time, it went unnoticed by Jiten and everyone else. It was only when the wife heard and commented on it that Jiten realized that prior to this, the boy had never used any particular word to address either him or his wife. Jiten's two children were at first angry that anyone other than themselves should call their father Baba. The parents however kept quiet and eventually they too stopped grumbling.

Pokenmong was no longer restless like before. He worked hard at splitting sufficient firewood to last many days, kept all the water containers full at all times and rid the kitchen garden of weeds and pests. He even managed to bring some flower seedlings, the ones that the neighbours threw out of their gardens as surplus, and lovingly planted them in front of their house. Jiten's little cottage soon assumed the look of a very cosy home unlike earlier when the entire compound seemed to have been overtaken by weeds and general neglect. The flowers in the front garden, though only ordinary varieties like hibiscus, marigold and sunflowers, gave the house a festive look when they bloomed in their season. Pokenmong also repaired the bamboo fencing, re-plastered the mud walls and pestered Jiten to buy lime to whitewash them. He was reluctant at first but when the children also supported Pokenmong's idea, he gave in and one day he came home in a rickshaw carrying a tin full of lime. On a Sunday all four of them, Jiten, Pokenmong and the two children, Sunita and Babul, mixed the lime with water adding some blue powder used on white clothes, and began to paint the entire house, inside and out, with the magic mixture. Not to be outdone in enthusiasm, Jiten's wife, Senehi, decided to cook 'pulao' and chicken curry for lunch in honour of the occasion. Every one was in a terrific mood and the painting job was done by lunchtime. After a brief nap Jiten changed into his uniform and seeing this, without waiting for the usual nod, Pokenmong also put on a clean shirt.

'Where do you think you are going?' Jiten asked Pokenmong, who only smiled and began to comb his hair.

'Same place as you are,' he answered and without waiting for any rejoinder marched ahead in a determined manner. Jiten had lately noticed a certain cockiness in the boy and decided to speak to him in private regarding his behaviour.

That day, as they awaited the arrival and passage of the goods train, a long line of vehicles began to form behind the closed gate of the crossing. There were at least fifty trucks laden with men and materials and they were all white soldiers, some singing and some talking loudly in a strange language. Unable to contain his curiosity, Pokenmong slid past the barrier and approached the first vehicle. Jiten, intent on the signal post did not notice what the boy had done. Waving the green flag from his observation tower, he waited for the long train to go out of his sight and began to shout for Pokenmong to open the barrier gate on his side. But the boy was nowhere in sight even after Jiten opened his side of the gate. Cursing the boy under his breath he walked over and opened the barrier. The long line of vehicles with the foreign soldiers whirred past him and in one of the trucks he saw Pokenmong's grinning face trying to say something to him. But the truck was travelling too fast and he did not hear anything. The only thing he remembered was the happy face of his domestic servant now moving on to another sphere. That was the last he saw or heard about this boy, who had once called him 'Baba', until the morning when Babul came home shouting and waving a newspaper, 'Baba, Baba, see what is written here.' Jiten read the name but could not connect it to the smiling face that had whizzed past the crossing on that day when he had felt as if he had indeed lost a son.

The 'foreign' soldiers were Americans who had come to set up camp in the perimeter of the barely functional airfield to oversee the final evacuation of men and materials from the last allied command-post of the Indo-Burma campaign. Through gestures and a smattering of a few English words, Pokenmong had managed a ride with them. He had no idea what he was going to do when they reached the destination. All that he knew was that he had to find out what these 'white' people were like, if they were at all like ordinary people or were a species apart from anything he knew. As his initial curiosity wore off, it started getting dark and he did not know the way back to Jiten's house. He hung around for some time and hid behind some barrels to settle for the night. One of the night patrols heard a sound and shone his light on the frightened boy who crouched and turned himself into a ball, whimpering. He dragged the boy from his hiding place and brought him inside the camp. Sensing that he might be hungry the soldier made him a corned-beef sandwich and throwing a blanket at him went out. At first the boy was reluctant to try the strange-looking meal in his hand but being terribly hungry, he took a small tentative bite and found that he liked it! He finished it in no time and was soon fast asleep, wrapped in the smelly blanket.

The next morning, he told the first soldier he met that he wanted to work for the 'sahibs'. He was taken to the camp commander who asked him, 'What is your name?'

He replied, 'My name Pokenmong. I Naga.'

'What do you want?' To this he could not say anything. Again he was asked, 'What do you want?' The commander was getting exasperated and his first instinct was to boot him out of the camp. But he saw that the strange boy was trying to say something. So he asked again, 'What do you want?'

Pokenmong looked at the white man and began to march, shouting, 'left, right, left, right'. The commander burst out laughing and instructed his adjutant to assign to him whatever menial work needed to be done in the camp. Pokenmong did whatever he was assigned to do: stacking empty cartons, sweeping the paths, peeling potatoes, washing dishes, wiping tables. He did not require to be told twice; it was as if he was trying to prove to them that he was needed by them. It was the same tactic that he had used when he was working in the other households. When he left a place, it was because he wanted to and not because he was turned out. Seeing these white men had opened a whole new world to the homeless boy and he wanted to stay with them to learn more. When evening came no one thought of turning him out of the camp. Instead, the cook took him behind the kitchen and gave him a plate full of beef stew and bread. Later on, Pokenmong washed the pots and pans while the cook sprawled in a chair and smoked.

Within a few days, the commander forgot that he had actually wanted the boy out of the camp at all; he seemed so indispensable. Any errand to be done, it was, 'Call Pok-what?' They found it difficult to pronounce the full name and made it into Porky. Shoes needed to be polished, call Porky; vests needed to be washed, tell Porky. The camp rang out with come here Porky, go there Porky, run Porky and where are you Porky? Within a month, Pokenmong picked up the basic words and even some of the choice words which he often used without really understanding the meanings, to the delight of the camp for whom he had become something of a mascot. Pokenmong responded to his new name quite readily, but something was bothering him. He began to think: why should he do all the work all over the camp? And should he not ask for wages? But before he did that, he had to be 'needed' at one single place all the time, and must have a regular kind of assignment.

So he started to hang around the commander's hut; sweeping the surroundings immaculately, then picking up bricks from all over the camp to lay a neat little foot-path for the commander from his hut to the field office, some hundred meters away. This done, he began to scour the adjoining fields looking for plants and planted them around the hut. The commander was impressed by the boy's initiative and decided to make him an assistant to his orderly. Pokenmong's plan was working and soon if any one wanted his services, they had to ask the commander's orderly first. He was a fast learner and by watching the other man constantly, he learnt to tidy up the hut, polish the commander's shoes just the way he liked them and was always at his door anticipating the big man's commands. Instead of being at the beck and call of every one in the camp, he became the commander's Man Friday and how he enjoyed his changed status! He even thought of asking to be paid a regular wage.

A year had already gone by since that day when Pokenmong decided to hitch his fortune to the strangers in those huge trucks. Since then, he had learnt more of their language and their mannerisms. He learnt to say hi, good morning, goodnight, but good afternoon was always his weak point. Another thing which fascinated him was the machine the commander spoke to in his hut; every day after he went to his office, Pokenmong would look all over the thing to find out who or what was hiding inside the strange-looking instrument.

On Sundays, the commander would be gone for most part of the day and it was then that Pokenmong would venture outside the camp area and investigate what lay beyond. During one such outing, he stumbled on a small village of about twenty-odd houses where some farmers lived with their families. The villagers were suspicious at first, but when they learnt that the boy worked for the 'sahibs' in the airfield, they became very curious. They plied him with all kinds of questions: what the strange-looking men ate, how they treated him, were they really human beings? Pokenmong laughed at the questions and told them that the sahibs were 'just like us' and were in fact very good to him. He told them that he was the assistant to the 'burra sahib' and that he could enter his hut any time he wanted! The villagers were amazed at this boy's good fortune to be living and eating with the 'gora sahibs'. He was immediately taken to the gaonburah's house where he was once again quizzed by the elders. The villagers were living in anxiety given the proximity of the white men's camp; they did not know that the Great War was over. They were so jittery that whenever they heard the planes they all ran into the nearby jungles. Pokenmong assured them that they need not do that any more as the planes were merely transporting men and materials from the area and that very soon the whole camp would be gone. They listened to him attentively and requested him to come the next Sunday too with more news. The gaonburah's wife cooked a delicious meal and after what seemed like ages, Pokenmong had rice, daal and meat curry, which for a moment reminded him of Jiten's household. But he soon dismissed the thought and he began to think of what would happen to him after the white soldiers left the country. He realized that he had to plan for his own survival once again.

During the whole of the ensuing week, Pokenmong was distracted by his worry about the future and went about the camp like one who did not know where he was. The commander noticed this and called him one evening into his tent and began to question him as best as he could; though the young man had become fairly conversant with English, he lacked the vocabulary for any serious talk. The commander asked him,

'What is wrong, Porky? You sick?'

'No sahib, no sick here,' pointing to his body, 'but sick here,' holding his head.

'Why Porky, why?'

'You go, all go, and Porky no go. Porky go where? Porky no house, no village, no mommy, no daddy. You my daddy, after Jiten baba. But Jiten baba angry, Porky run away. Porky mad, mad.' And he began to whimper like a wounded animal.

The white man was perplexed at this turn of events. He had hardly thought of Porky as capable of thinking about the future. Sure he liked the boy and admitted that it was very convenient to have him around the camp but beyond that, he did not spare a moment's thought to the future of the boy who had become a fixture in his camp. Try as he would, he could not find words to console the distraught boy, so he merely patted him and said, 'We'll talk tomorrow, Porky. Goodnight.' Porky had learnt that 'goodnight' was a signal for dismissal and so with bowed head he went out of the tent towards his own quarters that he shared with the other menial staff.

He waited for a summons from the commander every evening, but in vain. So on Saturday night, he went to the commander's hut and knocked on the door. There was a gruff 'Come in' and when he saw Porky, he looked surprised. But he simply motioned for him to sit on a stool and continued writing. Porky waited and after what seemed like hours, the commander turned to him and began to speak, 'Look Porky, we are all going back to America in three days' time but we cannot take you with us. That's it boy, Porky no can go with sahib, do you understand?' Porky nodded, all the time looking at the white man as though at an apparition. The commander continued, 'See, I have written here that whatever we leave behind will be yours: clothes, shoes, utensils, furniture, food, tents, tires and even a jeep in running condition. Do you understand? But Porky no go with Americans.' Porky nodded again, this time with a new brightness in his eyes. The commander then called the boy towards him and gave him a bundle of notes, Indian currency which had become useless to them. By now Porky was definitely excited and he tried to execute a salute as he often saw the soldiers do. The white man seemed pleased that he had pacified Porky and somewhat eased his own conscience. Pokenmong's career as a camp-hanger was thus terminated by the piece of paper that he held in his hand; it made him the inheritor of the abandoned camp in an almost defunct airfield.

So the remnants of the foreign fighting forces loaded their pride and glory in war-weary aircraft and left the desolate camp to a bewildered youth with a sheet of paper carrying the insignia of the conquerors telling him that he was now lord and master of the vacant space and the debris that littered it. Pokenmong moped around the camp for two whole days, did not keep his appointment with the villagers and stared at the paper, trying to make out what the scribbling meant. He ignored the left-over gifts, the food rotted, and suddenly the camp was swamped by hordes of ants, rats and raucous crows which materialized out of nowhere. In the evenings, jackals who had previously been kept at bay by the soldiers' guns, emboldened by the silence in the camp, roamed freely.

On the third day, Pokenmong woke up with a new resolve: he would go to see the gaonburah and try to strike a deal with the villagers; he would sell them all the things left by the Americans. But in order to convince them, he had to put up a very strong case why they should buy the property from him, the new owner. So he began to inspect the camp and commit to memory the more valuable items. He counted the number of beds, chairs, tables and kitchen utensils. Next came the footwear, usable blankets, shirts, sweaters; even odd things like photo-frames, mirrors, magazines and bags and suitcases of various sizes and shapes. All these, he knew, would be of instant interest to the villagers. Next, he thought about the jeep; he knew there was a man in the village who was handyman to a truck driver in the town and might be interested in the vehicle.

While he was mentally totting up this inventory, he began to doubt if the simple villagers would be interested in a pile of used goods left by some strangers. They might even reject the entire idea. The more he thought about this possibility, the more disturbed he became. But he was not willing to give up yet; he had to find a way to make some capital out of his stint with the Americans. He asked himself, what does an ordinary farmer value most? And the answer came to him instinctively: the land! He remembered now how his father used to talk and dream about owning more land to cultivate, and he understood that it was this frustration which had made him so ill-tempered. He believed that no farmer would scoff at an offer of land, to be had so easily. So he decided to play this card: he would sell the entire air-field and as a bonus, would give them everything else in it, including the jeep. It would be the biggest attraction for the villagers! He was jubilant; he believed that he had found the best argument to convince them. He lost no time and after a bath and a meal put together from some tins, he made for the village. It did not bother him that it was almost evening.

When he reached the village, the menfolk had just returned from their fields. After the preliminary pleasantries, he made for the gaonburah's cottage where he unfurled the precious document given to him by the commander and explained to the assembled farmers what he had in mind. At first the villagers were non-committal; some even went to the extent of doubting the veracity of Pokenmong's claim about what was written in the piece of paper. But the gaonburah's son who was studying in class VII in the town happened to be there and he was asked to read and translate the writing. Though he was not yet proficient in English, he did not want embarrass himself and looked for the word 'airfield' which would lend credence to his translation. To his delight and Pokenmong's relief, he found the word in three places in the document and assured the farmers that Pokenmong was telling the truth.

So the villagers went into a serious huddle and after long deliberation, decided to buy the airfield collectively and divide it later. They were not enthusiastic about the other stuff but Pokenmong said that they could have it anyway and left it at that. They argued late into the night regarding the cost of the land; the gaonburah said Pokenmong was asking an exorbitant amount; he replied that they were getting a good bargain, what with the land being adjacent to their village and not very far from the main road. They negotiated through the impromptu dinner prepared by the gaonburah's wife and endless cups of black tea. Towards the wee hours of the morning when the first cock crowed, the gaonburah quoted a sum to which, after some show of hesitation, Pokenmong agreed. Inwardly he too, was crowing because he was getting Rs 500 for a piece of land which did not really belong to him and which he believed he would never see again. The entire group then slept for a few hours and at daybreak the others went to their own homes while the gaonburah counted out the money from the village fund. Pokenmong was served a hearty breakfast of flattened rice with jaggery and a steaming cup of tea with milk and sugar. He pocketed the money and went out of the house into the unknown once again.

Trouble started when the villagers began to divide the land and started digging up the field. For a week or so their activities went unnoticed but one day an official-looking man appeared at the gaonburah's house and began asking questions. He was shown the piece of paper written by the camp commander and told that they had bought the airfield from a boy called Pokenmong. He asked, 'Where is he?' No one had the answer; they had not bothered to ask him where he was from or where he was going. When the official read the document he began to laugh and told the villagers that they were really and truly a bunch of idiots because the airfield had never belonged to this person who sold had it. All that the villagers could do was hang their heads in shame and regret and curse the boy who had sold them an airfield.

The Letter

There was an uneasy quiet in the village: the underground extortionists had come and gone and along with them the hard-earned cash the villagers had earned by digging the first alignment for a motorable road to their village. It was a work that had been assigned to them by the Border Roads Organization, after much lobbying and often acrimonious negotiations. The BRO had at first refused to out-source work to the villagers saying that they had enough manpower to dig the alignment by themselves. The villagers had countered by saying that since the road was being constructed through their land, as landowners they had to be involved in demarcating the route which, otherwise, might encroach on the territory of the neighbouring village, and which in turn might lead to unnecessary complications. The contract was eventually awarded to them and they completed the work two days ahead of time. All those engaged in the work had different plans about spending the cash. A few of them wanted to put tin roofs on their houses; some had already entered into negotiations to buy pairs of bulls to plough their fields. One man had actually taken some planks from a neighbour on credit to repair his floor and was going to pay him off after he received his wages from the BRO.

What the villagers did not reckon with was the efficiency of the underground intelligence network.

On the very day that they were paid, some strangers entered their village at dusk. They ordered the frightened villagers to take them to the headman's house where they stated their demand. They read out the names of the villagers involved in the work and found one man was missing from the group. He was the same man who had bought the timber and was busy cutting it to size to repair the rotten floorboards. He was hauled in before the visitors who berated him soundly for ignoring their summons. The villagers sensed immediately that their plans for utilizing the hard-earned cash would come to nothing because they knew that these fierce-looking goons from the forest had come to the village at night with only one purpose: to rob them in the name of the underground government. Resisting them was of no use: they carried guns and the consequences of any conflict would only mean retaliation.

Such acts of blatant extortion from the so-called 'national workers' was not a new thing for the simple villagers. What amazed them was the timing of their arrival and the accuracy of their information. They even had records of how much each labourer had received from the BRO! Now, in the presence of the headman they began to read out how much each man had to pay them as 'tax'. With hatred in their hearts and murder in their eyes the men started to count the amounts due from each and placed them in front of the headman. But one man was counting his money again and again. When he had done it several times he began to appeal to the leader, saying that he had to pay off his debt to the timber trader and if he gave them his due, he would not be able to send any money to his son who was to appear in the final examination of the year and needed to pay the examination fee within the week. He promised to pay them soon but requested that he be excused from the present reckoning; otherwise his son would not be able to sit for the examination. This man had worked for fewer days because of his wife's illness and hence was paid the least amount. He even tried to explain this to the leader. But before he could complete the appeal, one of the extortionists shot out from the stool he was sitting on and hit the poor man with the butt of his rifle, 'What examination, what fees? Don't you know what sacrifices we have made in our fight against the government? And how we are suffering in the forest? Are you saying that we should not collect taxes so that your sons can give examinations and become big "babus" in the Indian government to rule over us?'

Even as he uttered the word 'Indian' his face seemed to distort with naked rage, like a fierce animal at the sight of an adversary. With the quickness born out of living in hostile surroundings, the headman pulled the fallen man aside, otherwise murder would have taken place at the very next moment. He also took the money from the injured villager and gave it to the still-angry man, asking him to leave immediately. Though the leader acted like he was offended by the tone of the headman, he complied because on many occasions he had been saved from the army patrolling parties by this man's advance warnings about their movements.

After the departure of the unwanted guests, the men began to administer first aid to the injured man. His face was already swelling, and his mouth and nose were bleeding. After cleaning him up as best as they could, they carried him to the village 'compounder' (pharmacist) who gave him some pills to stop the bleeding and told him to rest for a few days. In the meantime, the headman realizing the plight of this unfortunate man, lent him some money which was sent to his son studying in a nearby town, to take care of his examination needs. Though the immediate danger was avoided, the villagers were apprehensive about the presence of underground elements in the vicinity of their village. Lately, news had filtered in about the rogue elements in the movement who had taken to harassing simple villagers and townsfolk alike by 'collecting taxes' in the name of the underground government and using the money to feed their drug and drinking habits. There were even stories of how such characters were 'punished' by their superiors: with their hands and feet tied, they were shot in the head at point-blank range. What happened to these renegades was of little consequence to the villagers who knew that they had to contend with not only these different types of underground elements but also with government agents and the Indian army.

The people of this village were generally known to be docile, trying their best to avoid conflict with both the overground and the underground governments. They were also on fairly good terms with the army personnel who came to their village occasionally to buy vegetables, rice and other farm produce. But this incident seemed to have revived a somnolent rage in their minds. In groups of twos and threes they began to discuss their grievances over a number of days. At home, in fields and in forests their minds were filled with resentment and anger at the injustice inflicted on them over the years by the various players in Nagaland's murky politics, plunging Naga society into anarchy. As though driven by a hidden force, they converged on the headman's house one evening and began a heated discussion. The elderly were more cautious and urged restraint. But the younger ones spoke for action against these forces and asked for retaliation, at whoever henceforth treated them with disrespect and tried to 'steal' from them. The debate continued till the wee hours and the voice of the elders was drowned in the strong current of anger and resentment of the young. The village council finally resolved that they would cease to pay any 'tax' to the underground, would refuse to do 'free' labour for the government, and would discourage the army visits by refusing to sell any of their produce to them. This decision seemed to appease the anger of the youth and, with the first cock's crow, the assembly dispersed to their respective homes. Till the end however, the elders cautioned the youth not to initiate any unprovoked hostility.

In spite of the resumption of apparent normalcy in the village, the story of the assault on the hapless man evoked strong reactions even from the women. In private they called their menfolk 'women' and taunted them by indirect remarks and bawdy songs about their emasculation. The men could do nothing about this because in their hearts they acknowledged the fact that they had indeed been cowed down for a very long time. But these emotional upheavals were soon overshadowed by everyday realities and the village once again returned to its placid ordinariness.

The calm however was not to last long because when they least expected it, the inevitable happened.

It presented itself in the form of an armed man in the village asking for directions to the headman's house. The old woman who was thus accosted stood rooted to the spot. She had just come out of her son's house where she had gone to give a special dish that she had cooked for an ailing grandchild. Though old and seemingly out of touch with the current events of the village, she had lived in 'grouping zones' during the peak of the insurgency movement and survived beatings at the hands of the army. She had also seen the tortured victims, the so-called 'sympathizers' of the underground forces, and lived through the trauma in the wake of her husband's abduction and eventual killing by the underground on charges of being an informer and 'guide' of the Indian army. But this moment was epiphanic because, in spite of the camouflage uniform and scraggly beard, she recognized the man as one of the abductors of her husband. Squinting her eyes to pretend near-sightedness and keeping her voice as calm as possible she gave him directions, not to the house of the headman but to that of one of the members of the younger group.

After he left, she retraced her steps to her son's house to inform him of what she had done. He in turn grabbed his shawl and dao and sprinted to his friend's house in order to collect the group. Then a group of seven men was seen marching towards the house where the stranger was confronting the owner, brandishing his gun and threatening him that if he did not collect a certain amount of money as 'emergency tax' imposed by the underground army he would kill him and his family and any one who opposed him. Even as he finished saying this, he became aware of the group of villagers who surrounded him. Though he had the gun, he became terribly worried. Trying to put up a brave front, he challenged the newcomers, 'Who are you and why have you come here like this?'

At this, one of the group who was simply called Long Legs because of his height, countered his question with, 'We should be asking *you* that,' and so saying tried to advance towards him. The stranger, by now thoroughly frightened by the menace surrounding him, fired his gun. But luckily the bullet only whizzed past one of the villagers and no one was injured. The sound of gunfire in the meantime brought many other villagers out of their homes, at first very cautiously, but when word spread that there was only one underground man they all made for the house in front of which the fracas was in progress. Seeing so many able-bodied men surrounding him, the man tried to run away but his way was blocked by the human wall. No one knew for sure who started the beating but it continued mercilessly for several minutes until the man lost consciousness and slumped on the ground in a bloody heap. Realizing the gravity of the situation, the rest of the villagers deserted the scene leaving the young activists with the injured man, inert and bleeding profusely.

The owner of the house was by now almost incoherent with fear about the consequences of this incident and begged the group to remove the body as far away from his house as possible. Long Legs, the obvious leader of the group, instructed the others to lift the man. Telling them to follow him, he led them away from the village into a jungle path leading towards a ravine which was believed to be haunted by the ghost of a man who had fallen from a tree and dashed to his death on the stones below. It would soon be dark and the others protested that it was unsafe for them to venture into this unholy area. But he kept going, using his dao to clear the shrubbery on the trail. After much disgruntled huffing and puffing, the men reached a high point of the hillock with their burden.

Dumping the still-breathing man unceremoniously, the men sprawled on a clearing to rest awhile. They first made a bonfire in the middle with the dry wood and twigs lying nearby. It was obvious to every man what should happen to the inert body, but the question uppermost in everybody's mind was: how would it be done and what should they do afterwards? Long Legs himself seemed to be pondering on the question: he was pacing around the body, his eyes riveted to the ground. Sensing that any delay would only cause more difficulties for them, he called the others together and asked them the one question: should they leave the man to die where he was or should they hurl him down the cliff? The answer was unanimous: throw him down the cliff. Then what about his gun? That too, they replied. As the men were going to execute their decision, Long Legs cried out, 'Stop, let us at least find out who he actually was.' Once again the men let go of the body; he started rummaging through the pockets of the stranger and pulled out a few sodden notes of small denominations, a tattered ID with almost illegible writing and a letter addressed to a postbox of a nearby town. Having emptied the pockets, once again the men lifted the bloody heap which was once a man and to a collective count of three, hurled it to its final resting place. His gun too, was tossed after him. This done, the men sat down once again as Long Legs examined each scrap of paper. He counted the notes and found that the man had exactly forty-nine rupees. The ID was unreadable, so was another piece of paper which also seemed to have been a letter once. Then he began reading the letter with the postbox number: As he continued reading, his face began to change and he slumped to the ground as though struck by something heavy. His mates, however, physically tired and drained of emotions, failed to observe the sudden change in Long Legs's demeanour. The gathering dusk also helped. The entire group seemed to be in some kind of stupor.

Long Legs was the first to recover; he picked up all the contents from the dead man's pocket and threw them into the dying fire. As the group watched the paper-pile disappear in the smoke, each of them felt as if a huge burden had been lifted from his shoulders. After taking an oath that they would never reveal what had happened to the stranger, they began walking towards the village in the gathering darkness with the help of torches made of bamboo and reeds.

The letter was Long Legs's personal cross as long as he lived. Though he had never been a good student he remembered every word of it, the letter from the dead man's son, begging the father to send his exam fees.

Three Women

Prologue

A young man is hovering near the doorway of a humble cottage in a village. He can hear the happy chatter of several women who had assisted at the birth. Some of them leave after a while, greeting him with broad grins. Only three women, standing near the bed, are left. He wants to see the baby but their backs obstruct his view; he can only wait. These three women, though distinctly different, are linked through a mysterious bond that transcends mere blood ties.

Martha's Story

I am Martha and this is my story, of how I am different and not really so at the same time. When I was a little girl living with my mother and grandmother in a village in the hills, the other children used to call me 'coolie' and laugh at my dark complexion and strange features. After play I would come home and sometimes ask my grandmother why the other children called me 'coolie'. She used to shrug her shoulders and say, 'Just ignore them, they are jealous because you can run faster and throw the sticks higher.' I would be pacified and would soon forget what had happened at play. Grandmother's explanation helped me to endure their taunts.

Something else was different about me: my hair. It was thick and curly and because of this lice loved my head. No matter how hard my mother and grandmother tried to catch them with their bare hands and kill them between their thumbnails, they kept crawling all over my head, which itched all the time. It became so bad one summer that they got hold of a pair of scissors and

63

chopped off my hair. You should have seen the number of lice that crept out of the shorn hair and dotted the floor. My mother poured hot water on the lot and swept them off the floor and into the fire, hair and all. My, how the fire cackled that time!

The taunts of the boys and girls began once again when I was enrolled in school. They did not want to sit near me or play with me. Every time I stood up to ask for permission to go out, they would giggle. Sometimes even the teacher could not control their behaviour and that added to their amusement. But I was tough even then and I wanted to show them that I was smarter than all of them, and I learnt my lessons well: I was attentive in class and the teacher began to notice my progress. I remember very clearly what she told my mother when I was in class III, 'Medemla, this child of yours is very clever. One day she will become someone.' My mother only smiled but I kept wondering what she meant by 'someone'? By the time I was in class IV, some girls became quite friendly with me and I was very happy to have them as my friends. But the word 'coolie' had stuck in my mind and one day I asked them, 'Why do you all call me "coolie"?' They looked at each other and turned their faces away. After some whispering among them, the one called Chubala said, 'Don't you know that you do not belong to our village and that Medemla is not your real mother? Haven't you ever wondered why you look so different from us? You speak just like we do but it is not your language. Our mothers have always known this and they told us.'

I felt as if I had fallen into a dark hole. I did not know what to say, so I ran all the way home and sat on my small bed. When grandmother peeped in to see if I was all right, I blurted out in an angry voice, 'Tell me, who *is* my real mother?' She was caught unawares and withdrew hurriedly. But I would not let her go so easily. I followed her and shouted the question to her once again.

She did not look at me but sat on a low stool by the fireside with her head bent low. I stood near her for a while and, looking at that dejected figure, I felt a terrible loneliness. If this woman was not my grandmother and her daughter was not my real mother, whom did I have to call my own? Where did I belong and who were my people? And how did I become my mother's daughter and this old woman's granddaughter? With these thoughts, the sense of loneliness only grew stronger. So I inched my way to where grandmother was sitting and squatted near her. I always liked to smell her: the peculiar odour of her body was so different from all other scents. She smelt like the earth after rain or the smoke from burning wood and sometimes even like crushed leaves. I smelled these when she used to carry me on her back with the help of a cloth, tying the ends firmly across her chest so that I would not fall off. When I laid my head on her back, her warm body smell had a soothing effect on me and even though I might have been crying before, the contact with her body always put me at ease. How secure I used to feel then! At other times, whenever I got a sniff of these smells, I knew that grandmother was near and that I need not be afraid of anything. But sitting close to her that day, instead of the usual sense of security and comfort, I became afraid because, being different, I might be sent off to some place where I actually belonged. The fear of the truth that I was different from my grandmother and her daughter who was my mother was beginning to gnaw at my heart like the black lice of my childhood which had made my life so miserable. And this time I was not sure whether my mother and grandmother would help me get rid of this misery.

All that I thought of sitting next to my grandmother was that I did not want to be different because I did not *feel* any different from them or all the others in the village. At that moment I wanted to scrape off my dark skin and rearrange my strange features. I wanted to look like them because I always felt, thought and spoke like them. Grandmother continued sitting silently and I was growing restless with fear thinking that I would be sent back to my 'real' people and would never see my mother, grandmother or my new friends. I did not want to be sent away, I wanted to be in this village, with all the familiar faces, speaking the same language, going to the same school and doing everything together.

In the meantime it was getting dark and mother had not returned from her work in the government dispensary. And I was beginning to feel hungry. I looked at my grandmother to see what she was doing. She had closed her eyes and was mumbling some words under her breath, almost oblivious of my presence there. After what seemed like a long time, she got up slowly and said to herself, 'It's time to feed the pigs and chickens.' Once again I was plunged into despair, interpreting this as her way of dismissing me. But I sat on and decided that no matter what they, my mother and grandmother, did, I would resist being sent away and would insist that I belonged with them and that I was not in any way different from them. Thinking about what to say to mother when she came home, I found myself becoming angry and resentful towards these two older women who had withheld the truth from me, even though I admitted that they had shown only love and concern for me all this time. But I kept on asking myself: why had they not told me the truth?

Medemla's History

I am Martha's mother but the real story of my life began long before her birth, on the day I received that terrible letter from Imsutemjen, my long-time fiancé, telling me that he could not marry me because his father was vehemently opposed to the idea. I still cannot describe the feeling of rejection and betrayal that seemed to incinerate me, reducing me to nothingness. I began to wonder if there was anything peculiar or different in me that repelled his father. It took the better part of a year for me to come out of the depression which set in. Only because of the heavy workload as a resident nurse in the hospital where I trained that I was able to outwardly maintain some semblance of normalcy. My father was terribly hurt by this unexpected turn and came to see me. But my mother simply sent word through him that I should consider myself fortunate in not marrying such a man. Though there were good proposals after the break-up, I rejected every single one without a qualm, much to the consternation of my parents. They were shocked that I would do such a thing, especially in a case or two where they had tentatively given their consent to the boys' parents. When it became apparent to everyone, my parents included, that I was determined to remain single, they simply left me alone.

And then Martha came into my life as though ordained by some unknown powers. I happened to be the staff nurse in the maternity ward and had to oversee every delivery. Generally, people have the habit of coming to hospitals as a last resort when all home remedies fail and quacks wash their hands off, citing God's will. We were able to help save many such cases in our ward but there was the occasional failure where a patient died through totally unforeseen causes. Martha's mother was such a case. When she was brought to us she had lost much blood and was near collapse. If the baby was not delivered soon, we were afraid that both mother and child would die. But the husband would not consent to a Caesarean section; so the failing woman had to be given inductive drips and was made to exert some more to push the baby out. Luckily, the delivery was accomplished and the healthy baby began to squeal the moment she was born. Then disaster struck: the mother went into convulsions and before the doctor could be summoned, she died.

I have never felt such a sense of failure as I did that day. No matter how much I tried to convince myself that it was a hopeless case from the very beginning, I somehow felt personally responsible for the tragedy; that in the joy of delivering a living child we had somehow neglected to detect the tell-tale signs of some serious problem in the woman's weakened body. When the husband heard the news, he broke down and cried like a baby. But when he learned that the child was a girl, his entire demeanour changed. He stood up in a rage and railed against the nurses, the hospital and above all against a cruel God who had denied him a son. When he was asked what he was going to do about the baby girl, he shot back, 'What will I do with another girl? Do whatever you want; I don't want to see her ever, she who has killed my wife.'

This is how Martha became a ward of the hospital and an addition to the group of abandoned children who would either be adopted or brought up by the Mission. The name Martha was given to her by one of the nurses after the father disowned her. From the very beginning there was something about this baby who had caused so much anguish to people on her entry into the world. For some inexplicable reason I became attached to her from those early days and when she started to coo and smile, my heart was captured by the serenity and beauty of her smile. Even after I was shifted from that ward, I used to visit her every day before going home. She began to recognize me and would cry when I left. It was as if some unseen hand was forging a bond between my lonely self and this abandoned child and inwardly, I began to dread the day when some childless couple would adopt and take her away from my life. That is how I began to examine the possibility of adopting her myself.

At first it seemed like a preposterous idea, even to me! Imagine a single unmarried woman, still completing the obligatory internship in the hospital, unsure of future placement either in this very hospital or elsewhere, daring to think of adopting an orphan girl. But above all these practicalities stood the hurdle of genetic and cultural disparity. I was an Ao-Naga, of medium height, fair complexion and still young at twenty-six. And Martha? Dark as a bat, with distinctly aboriginal features and a head of thick curly hair already showing signs of an Afro! I was all too aware of these obstacles but strangely, they only reinforced my desire to take this child and make her my daughter.

I then decided to write to mother asking her if she would look after this child I was planning to adopt until I fulfilled my obligation to the hospital. In my letter, I gave only the barest details about Martha, wilfully omitting the physical description, only highlighting the mother's tragic death and the father's blunt and harsh refusal even to look at his own flesh and blood. I was not very optimistic about my mother's response because I did mention the fact that Martha's parents belonged to the tea tribe. It was nearly a month before mother replied saying that if such a step would make me happy, she was willing to take the child to the village and look after her until I found a regular job.

I was ecstatic over this positive response and went immediately to the Nursing Superintendent with my proposal. She listened in silence and dismissed me with a curt reply, 'Think over it seriously and come back in a week's time.' I was terribly disappointed and also confused; these people who always taught us about loving the unfortunate, ugly and sick people of the world seemed to disapprove of my wish to adopt an abandoned child. But I would not give up and went to her earlier than she had suggested. I told her about the arrangement with my mother for looking after the child until I finished my stint in the hospital. This time, the Super was ready with the terms: if I insisted on adopting Martha, she told me, I would have to leave my job immediately and would get no letter of reference from the hospital. I was stunned! They were going to punish me for doing something which they always preached. If they thought that this would sway my decision about adopting Martha, they were sadly mistaken. It only made me more adamant in my resolve. I told the Super that I still wanted to go through with the adoption and not only that, they should pay me for the number of days that I had already worked that month.

From a fellow nurse I came to know that some people from my village who had come to visit a relative in the hospital were leaving in a few days' time and I arranged to leave with Martha in their group. It was indeed a fortuitous coincidence because the fag end of the journey to our village after getting off the train would be on foot. And these kind people took turns in carrying the little baby on their backs when I became too tired to go any further. And so I stepped into my father's house with a baby on my back while a fellow traveller carried my few belongings into the cottage.

The first reaction of my parents on seeing Martha was one of shock, disbelief and even of open disgust. But after a good night's sleep when they saw her in daylight and the child bestowed her first smile on them, they were completely mesmerized: they simply gawked at her and their faces broke into genuinely happy smiles.

They clamoured to hold her but the child was reluctant to go to them at first. It was mother who succeeded in making friends with Martha within the first week and she started to carry her on her back wherever she went. Her trips to the fields became less frequent and after a while stopped altogether. If father remonstrated, she would reply curtly, 'What, you're going to baby-sit her when I am away in the field?' He had no answer to this and with the ease born out of organizing household affairs, mother established the routine that continued until Martha was enrolled in school in her fifth year. She was a good student and sailed through every exam with excellent marks and I secretly began to dream of sending her to medical college to become a doctor. But I had reckoned without the independent spirit which she exhibited from the earliest days.

When I came home that day exhausted from a difficult delivery case, I found them, my daughter Martha and my mother, sitting sullenly silent and strangely, away from each other. They had not lighted the lamp nor started the evening meal. Their silence was catching; I too sat down near them without saying anything. It was mother who uttered the first words, 'Medemla, tell your daughter whether you are her real mother or not.' I looked at this young girl whom I called daughter and began to tell her the history of her birth and subsequent adoption and asked her in the end, 'So now, don't you think that I am your mother though in a different way?' My daughter, with all her intelligence could not articulate her response to such an adult question and my mother chided me for creating more confusion in her mind. She started to say something and this time I stopped her, 'Let her give an answer which will be the answer to her own question.' Martha stood up, as though she were in school and coming closer to us said in a clear voice, 'Mother, I may look different from you or grandmother or from all others in the village but I *feel* no difference in my heart.' She could not continue and broke down in sobs. I went closer and embracing her, said, 'Just as you feel, I am your real mother. Do you understand?' She nodded through her tears and I could see that there were tears in my mother's eyes also as she put her arms around us.

The three of them just stood there for quite some time; a strange trio, as though enacting a ritualistic affirmation of the power of mother-love to mesh the insecurity of innocence in the magic of an emotionally enlarged truth.

Lipoktula's Secret

My name is Lipoktula and I am Martha's grandmother. You may wonder why I do not begin by saying 'I am Medemla's mother.' It is because my role as grandmother to this alien child is not encumbered with any sense of guilt or fear whereas my role as Medemla's mother was. Our life was difficult, our sole resources were what we grew in our fields and that was not much. The additional income came through my weaving and my husband's wages as a daily labourer in odd places after our harvests were over. Even then we could not meet with the deadlines for paying fees, and the older boys sometimes could not sit for exams. In disgust both of them ran away and joined the Assam Rifles, after studying only up to class VI. Medemla's case was different; she was very good in studies and there was no problem about her fees because the boys used to send us money regularly. She went on to do her matric exam and then decided to go to nursing school. She was a good girl; obedient, humble and not at all flighty like some of her age-set. I was confident that one day she would make an excellent wife and a good mother. Little did I know how her future would be blighted by the secret of my past.

The nightmare started the day I received a letter from Medemla telling me of her friendship with a boy from our village who was studying to be an engineer in the same town where she was undergoing training. She went on to say that she had fallen in love with this boy named Imsutemjen, son of Merensashi, a council member of our village, and informed us that they were planning to get married in the winter. The boy's father would soon approach her father and formally ask for her hand. I felt as if a bolt of lightning from the sky had struck me and I collapsed in a heap on the floor. Luckily I was alone at home that day when the letter was brought and I decided to destroy it immediately. I threw it into the fireplace and saw it crumple into a black mass and mingle with the ashes. I realized that my dark secret had at last raised its ugly head and was about to destroy two families and along with it, my daughter's happiness. This marriage had to be stopped. But how? What could I say to Medemla or even to the boy? And above all, could I ask my husband to refuse permission without citing a convincing reason? The only person who could break up this relationship was the boy's father.

I thought of this the whole night and decided that I had to confront the man who was responsible for making me carry this secret in my heart for all these years. You see, Merensashi had raped me many years ago and Medemla is his child. It happened like this. His field adjoined ours and one day when my husband was away on a road construction job, he came in while I was eating the mid-day meal, claiming that he had stumbled and may have sprained his ankle. I finished my food hurriedly and boiled water to give him hot fomentation for his injured foot, though I noticed that he was looking at me in that certain way that a man does when he is sexually interested in a woman. All the same, I finished my task and was about to go back to my field, when he stretched out his hand as though to thank me and pulled me to the ground. I did try to ward him off but he was like an enraged bull and his passion was brutal. When he was done, he held on to me and would not let go of my body lying almost naked next to him. He tried to say something and I began to collect my clothes in order to slip out and make for the village. But no, something stirred in him and he pinned me to the ground and took me once more.

When he rolled off me the second time, visibly spent, I grabbed my clothes and sprinted out of the hut and made a detour to the stream to wash myself thoroughly. It was when I was squatting in the water to wash out what he had poured into me that I realized what had happened to me. Though I started to blame the man, there was a recurrent question in my mind: why had I not resisted more vigorously, screamed or even scratched his face when he was groping for my sex? I could not explain my own conduct. But the fact remained that it had happened, not only once but twice in the space of half an hour, and here I was sitting in water like a fool to wash it off! And I began to condemn myself. I sat in the water for a long time as though to wash away the sense of shame and guilt now overtaking me. It was only when I felt numb due to the cold that I came out, dried myself, dressed and made for home, a thoroughly confused and broken woman. For many days I remained at home, pretending to be sick, and did not stir out of the house. Then I missed my period and soon realized that I was pregnant. The burden on my soul was becoming unbearable, and in the second month, I went to my mother and blurted out the truth to her. She chided me for not running away immediately but all the same, was absolutely heartbroken at my plight, and we both cried hard and long. In the end she said to me, 'You know, it is always wise for a woman to keep a part of the self all to herself and sometimes she has to choose between telling the truth which destroys, and living with a lie which may remain a secret forever. I cannot say anything more because it is only you who can make the choice.' That day I made a momentous decision: I would remain silent.

It never occurred to me not to have the baby and Medemla was born, to the delight of my husband who had always longed for a daughter. I admit I was terrified at times but hoped that no one would ever come to know the truth about this child's true parentage. She would always belong in our family. When Medemla was about a year old, my mother took a long intense look at her and whispered, almost to herself, 'Thank god, she does not look too different from her brothers.'

But she was different from them, and, I had to think long and hard about the terrifying spectre of an incestuous marriage. I realized that the onus was entirely on me to prevent it at all costs even though it would mean destroying my own daughter's prospects of happiness in the process. I agonized over the pain that my daughter would feel if the marriage was called off. But there was no earthly way of avoiding this seeming act of cruelty against my own child which must be carried out in order to avert the curse of incest. Hurting her just this once was, in my mind, far better than seeing her in an incestuous marriage forever. 'No one would know' had worked once to cover my guilt from my husband. But if I took refuge in this now, it would mean committing a graver crime not only against my own flesh and blood but also against a society where such marriages are banned; in ancient times the penalty was death. The first time I had acted out of fear of the truth which would have ruined two families. But now I was going to build a defence on the truth because of a different kind of fear: the fear that my daughter would be condemned to live in an incestuous marriage.

I had to work out a strategy through which I could privately urge the boy's father to oppose the marriage. So the next Sunday when Merensashi walked out of the church, I stepped in beside him as though two churchgoers were walking back home side by side, quite by accident. At a point where there was no one near, I quickly informed him of his son's intent to marry Medemla and told him that if he did not stop it, I would publicly announce that he had fathered Medemla that day in the hut and that his blood ran in her veins. He was not convinced at first that she was his child, so I told him, 'She has a birthmark below her left collar-bone, just like yours. Besides, I should know when she was conceived.' Saying what I had to say, I walked away.

I do not know exactly what happened but soon after this, Imsutemjen wrote a curt letter to Medemla breaking off the engagement, and the rest is her history.

Martha

Mother wanted me to become a doctor: it would mean that I had to be away from the village for many, many years to complete my studies. I did not want to be away for so long from the village where now I felt I truly belonged. Every one treated me as an equal and nobody mentioned the word 'coolie' in my presence any more. Besides, I had fallen in love with my classmate Apok and we planned to marry when we finished our eighth class. We were secretly meeting every weekend in grandmother's barn mainly to talk, but the intimacy of being together away from anybody's gaze emboldened us and before we realized what we were doing we started to make love. Though he was gentle and kind, I cried a little the first time because he hurt me there. I had some initial misgivings about what we were doing, but Apok's gentle ardour overwhelmed me each time and soon I began to look forward to these exciting encounters. I was going to tell my mother soon about our relationship, but before I could do that, something happened: I became pregnant. When I told her, she turned to me with an ashen face and said, 'Martha, Martha, what have you done? Why couldn't you have waited? I was going to arrange a grand wedding for you. Instead, you have brought shame upon the family by becoming pregnant before the wedding. There will not be a proper wedding now, only a small gathering of relatives and the Pastor to formalize your marriage to Apok.' I looked at her pained expression and wondered: how could one describe the responses of a woman's body to the touch of a man she loved to such a person as my mother, who had never felt the demanding power of such love? And harder still, convince her that once you've tasted love like that, there was no stopping?

Medemla

I am both shocked and amazed at what has happened to Martha. In a way I am glad that my father is not here to face this; he died suddenly when Martha was in her fourth class. Now that everything is out in the open, these two youngsters have become inseparable and openly display their love and desire for each other. I keep asking myself: what is it that pulls a man and woman together and makes them so irresistible to one another? Why did I never feel that way with Imsu? And when I think back to the time after Imsutemjen's rejection of me, I realize that whatever sense of dejection and abandonment I had felt at that time, it was somehow not personal or intimate; but more like the disruption of an order of things that ought to happen in a woman's life. And after this debacle, I decided that I would have nothing to do with any man, ever. This has often led me to ask myself: Am I abnormal or just a different kind of woman?

Lipoktula

Medemla came to tell me about Martha's pregnancy and ask me what should be done. I told her that we should now formalize their relationship as soon as possible. And then she did a strange thing. In the middle of our planning for the home ceremony, she blurted out, 'Mother, I don't understand why they had to do it before marriage. Could they not have waited? What is it that drove them to it? I can tell you now that I never felt like that with Imsu even when we were alone.' How could I explain to her why the law of attraction between a man and a woman could not apply to them, and why she had not felt that way with Imsu? Even an old woman like me still remembers and understands the inevitable force that draws a man and a woman towards one another. Since she had never entertained any other man's overtures, Medemla would never experience the impulse that draws a man and a woman into that kind of intimacy.

Though I have told you that I was raped by Merensashi long ago, even now, when I recall the encounter, I remember, much more than my sense of outrage, the absurd power of his sex in overcoming my initial protest. Just as my mother did, I too have asked myself many times why I had not run out the moment I understood what this intentions were that day. But each time, I only recall how contagious the crazed passion of the man was

and how an inexplicable reaction of my body turned my feeble
resistance to participatory submission.

Epilogue

'Push!' they urge her, and she tries one more time to heave but nothing
happens. Her scream rings out in the night and Apok comes rushing in, only
to be pushed back outside. 'Stay there,' is the command, adding, 'if you can't
bear to hear her cry, go far away.' But he hangs around; the labour has been
going on for almost twelve hours and even Medemla the experienced nurse is
despairing: would it be a tragedy for Martha also? There is a short lull in
between the pains and Martha asks for some water, but before she can gulp
down the first mouthful, a massive wave of pain overtakes her body, making
her almost arch convex from the cot. The growl she emits is like nothing these
women who have participated in many deliveries, have ever heard, and as the
last hiss leaves her throat, one of them shouts, 'I see the head, one more
push, baby, just once more.' Martha hears her and with an ultimate effort
gives another push and the baby slithers out of her exhausted body. The
baby's wet and slimy contours as it surges through the passage produces such a
sensuous effect on Martha that she will always remember it as more sublime
than the transient ecstasies of sex.

The new mother slumps on her bed totally spent, while the other women
busy themselves with the rituals following a birth. When the child is brought
to her, Martha looks at it with awe, and thinks with a deep sadness of her
mother who has never experienced the pleasurable pains of motherhood.
The grandmother is watching Martha all throughout and gives her a
knowing wink. She picks up the baby and holds it out to Medemla. The
new mother turns to look at the two women as they encircle her child in
their arms. She thinks, they too, are mothers in their own ways and now she
has joined their ranks. The mother and the grandmother come to the bed

where she is resting and ceremoniously lay the baby next to her, in a ritualistic acknowledgement of her motherhood.

Apok, the new father, who is watching the activities of the women from the doorway, now comes forward, directing his gaze towards the bed in order to have a closer look at his just-born son. But his vision is obstructed by the daunting circle of the women, these three different kinds of mothers, standing as though mesmerized by the miracle of new life. He is reluctant to break the spell and, feeling like an intruder in a sacred ceremony, slips out unobserved.

A Simple Question

Imdongla woke up that morning with an uneasy feeling; she was sure she'd had a bad dream but could not remember what it was about. During her morning chores she tried to recollect it but without success; so she turned to her husband and told him of her foreboding, 'Listen, I've had a very weird dream, something bad will happen today. So don't shoot your mouth off like you always do and stay at home only.' He simply grunted at her and muttered, 'You and your dreams!' But Imdongla insisted, 'Just be careful, today is not a good day,' and left for the far-off field.

Imdongla was barely literate, able to read the Bible and the Hymn book only. But, she was otherwise a worldly-wise woman, knowledgeable about the history and politics of the village. She had grown up in a household where discussions about these were daily fare because her father was a gaonburah. Her husband, Tekaba, was also a gaonburah, and they had four healthy children. The gaonburahs were appointed by the government from the major clans as their agents to help maintain order in the village, and were issued a kind of uniform: red and black jackets and red blankets as symbols of their status. They worked in tandem with the traditional village council, also founded on the principle of clan representation. Set up during the British days, the system continued even after India gained independence.

If, during peacetime these elders enjoyed a privileged status, they became the most vulnerable ones when hostilities broke out between the Nagas and the Indian state. On the one hand, they were held responsible by the government if any young men from their villages were reported to have joined the rebel forces; on the other, the underground forces ordered them to identify young men representing each clan to join their army, failing which they threatened to burn down the village granaries. The forced 'conscription' was soon followed by 'demands' for material support like money, grain and livestock. Though the gaonburahs were supposed to inform the government about the activities of the rebels, they were under tremendous pressure from the underground forces because every move they made was monitored from close quarters. There were instances when certain elders suspected of being 'with' the government had been summarily executed. For the gaonburahs it was an extremely untenable situation.

The demand for 'taxes', as they were termed by the underground, started innocuously enough. The very first time it was Re 1 collected from every household to pay for the travel expenses of the rebel leader going to foreign lands to plead for Naga independence from India. At that time, Imdongla, though reluctant to part with hard-earned cash, however small the denomination, gave in without much protest. But as the years went by, the demands grew, and reluctance or protest was met with by severe beatings, not only of the person involved but of the gaonburahs and the elders as well. Several times it was Imdongla's presence of mind which had saved Tekaba from being beaten. Once the collectors had gathered in front of her house, and were berating a villager for bringing less rice than he was supposed to and asking him why he had dared disobey the command. The petrified villager could not say anything in his own defence. Imdongla was watching the unfolding scenario from the house. Then the leader turned to her husband Tekaba and said, 'What do you have to say about this?' At this point Imdongla decided that if she did not intervene both the men would be beaten mercilessly. Dashing inside, she grabbed a basket of freshly husked rice and came out shouting, 'Hey, Toshi, why don't you tell this man that I could not return this rice to you this morning as promised. Remember you lent it to my son for the age-set feast? Here it is.' So saying she set the basket on the ground and turned to the collector, 'You can see, brother, this is more than what he has to give, please take the lot and go, otherwise you will be caught in the rain.' The sky was indeed turning dark with rain-clouds. The man looked at her for some time, gestured to his soldiers to gather the rice and left the village at a running pace, leaving both her husband and the villager dumbstruck.

Very soon the entire land was gripped by terror unleashed both by the underground forces as well government soldiers. Within a couple of years of the commencement of hostilities, the army had established camps in strategic villages with regular patrols mounted every day for the safe passage of more soldiers into the interior of the land. Even in their village, an army camp was built on a hillock. Ironically, it was Tekaba and the elders of the council who accompanied the Deputy Commissioner of Mokokchung to officially hand over the prime site for the soldiers to set up their camp. As soon as the soldiers moved into their camp, a new sense of foreboding settled on the village. Whichever village allowed the setting up of army camp became prime suspects in the eyes of the underground and, as a form of punishment, were taxed double the amount. Resisting the coming of the army on the other hand was not an option because then the government itself would initiate measures to punish the un-cooperative village: all able-bodied men would be forced to work (without wages or food) in government projects like levelling a hillock to build a football field or clearing up to two hundred metres on both sides of the highway so that the underground soldiers would not be able to ambush army convoys, a regular occurrence. Villagers who persistently resisted the setting up of army camps would be forced out of their villages; their houses and granaries would be burnt and they would be relocated along with other recalcitrant villagers in a 'grouping' zone and kept in fenced-in areas, not allowed to cultivate their fields, their movements monitored and under constant surveillance.

The situation was steadily growing worse: from the meagre harvest the villagers had to meet with the demands of the belligerent 'collectors' of the underground. Now the taxes were in all three forms; rice, livestock and money. Sometimes all three would be demanded at the same time. Imdongla could see the effects of the terrible pressure on her husband; his hair had turned white, his face was gaunt with hunger and apprehension, and his eyes had a furtive look. He spoke little and tossed on his hard bed by the fireside all night. He even thought of resigning but Imdongla pointed out that if he so much as mentioned it to anyone the government would suspect him of being a sympathizer of the rebels and arrest him. Besides, she pointed out, everyone would call him a coward; how would he like that?

The double tax of rice from the underground brothers came during a particularly bad year; they had already collected the tax from the first harvest in August and now demanded another one from the winter crop. After the earlier lot had been paid, the army chaps led by a fierce-looking Havildar had come around asking all sorts of questions. The villagers pleaded ignorance and got away lightly with only some choice words from the leader. The second demand coming so close after the first put the elders in a quandary. They met in Tekaba's house and debated long into the night. Imdongla forcefully butted in to advise resisting the so-and-so's from the jungle. Tekaba tried to hush her, 'Keep quiet, woman, you know nothing.' At this she flared up, 'Know nothing? Well, who saved you the last time when you stood there like a statue about to wet your loin cloth? Just think how our daughter will feed her children if they take away what's left after paying their debt to the uncle!' And turning to the other men she continued, 'And you venerable elders, where is your wisdom? Your courage? Can't some of you go to the jungle and talk to the leaders? Plead with them? Haven't we always given them what they wanted? Ask them for time; instead of rice offer them some pigs and chickens. We can do without meat but we cannot live without rice. Don't you see what's happening to our children and women?'

The day on which she could not remember the bad dream of the previous night, Imdongla walked to the field thinking about the debate: she was sure that her dream had something to do with this. She resolved to tell her daughter to repay only half of what they owed so that after paying their due to the underground they would have enough rice for themselves to last till January; then her husband could look for work on the road-building projects or even in the army camp where they constantly needed labourers to mend fences or carry loads from the big trucks which brought supplies for them regularly. But when she reached home in the evening she was told that a group of soldiers had come and dragged all the elders including her husband to the army camp on charges of giving supplies to the underground. It was a cold night and to her surprise she saw that her husband's red blanket was lying in a corner. Knowing how susceptible he was to cold, she grabbed it along with his red and black jacket and started for the army camp. When she was leaving, her daughter came out of the inner room and said, 'The army man pulled it off father's shoulder saying that he did not deserve to wear it because he was supporting the jungle men.'

Imdongla walked resolutely towards the camp with the warm clothing bundled into a tight packet. When she reached the gate the sentry would not allow her in but she began to shout at him in her dialect pointing to the captain's hut and saying, 'Sahib, sahib.' The sentry gave in to her insistent muttering and thinking that she might be an informer, let her through. When she entered the hut there seemed to be no one around but she heard voices from a room beyond a partially open door. She peeped in and saw an enclosure of bamboo stakes where all the elders were being held captive. Only her husband was in a separate enclosure. As soon as she spotted him, she threw the blanket and jacket through the opening between the stakes. She was so quick that by the time the captain realized what was happening, Tekaba had put on the jacket and wrapped himself in the blanket. The captain turned to his soldiers and started to shout at them asking who had let this mad woman into the camp. He made as if to open Tekaba's cell but Imdongla jumped in between him and the make-shift lock-up, talking rapidly. The captain turned to someone in the shadows and asked him to interpret what she was saying. He told the captain that she had come to take her husband home and would not leave without him.

The captain saw that short of shooting her, there was no other way of getting rid of her. She sat in front of Tekaba's enclosure and when the captain approached her, she stood up and made as if to take off her waist cloth which he knew was the ultimate insult a Naga woman could hurl at a man signifying his emasculation. He turned round and went out of the room. Imdongla again squatted on the earthen floor and pulled out her metal pipe with a bamboo nozzle and filled it with home-grown tobacco. She saw a box of matches on the captain's table and crossed over to snatch it. She lit her pipe and dragging on it deeply, sat down to continue her vigil, tucking the matchbox in the folds of her supeti. She then stationed herself at Tekaba's cage-door. She had concluded that as long as she was there the soldiers would not dare beat up her husband and the other elders.

Outside, the captain was mulling over the other things the interpreter had told him. Imdongla had said, 'Look at them; aren't they like your own fathers? How would you feel if your fathers were punished for acting out of fear? Fear of you Indian soldiers and fear of the mongrels of the jungle.' But what affected him most was one single question that Imdongla had repeatedly asked: 'What do you want from us?' For the first time in his tenure in these hills, this apparently simple village woman had made him see the impossible situation faced by the villagers. Abruptly he turned to his adjutant and told him to release Tekaba and escort the couple beyond the perimeter of the camp. He however decided to keep the others overnight as a face-saving ploy for the army.

After the couple left, he felt restless and wanted a smoke to calm his nerves. He began looking for the matchbox he had kept on the table and which Imdongla had earlier appropriated. The captain was puzzled at first but suddenly remembered seeing the old woman smoking her pipe and concluded that she had stolen his matchbox and was freshly perturbed. The petty thievery which would normally have been ignored, once again reminded him how a coarse and illiterate village woman had managed to unsettle his military confidence by challenging the validity of his own presence in this alien terrain.

Sonny

I came home that fateful summer, out of a sense of filial duty, to spend a month with my ageing parents. Another reason that helped me decide on this journey was the apparent cessation of hostilities between the conflicting forces, maintained by a fragile cease-fire agreement. But there remained the bitter and violent rivalries among the different groups of freedom-fighters which often resulted in senseless deaths of leaders and cadres alike, creating a new sense of terror in the minds of the general public. The nagging misgivings about these sporadic killings notwithstanding, I came to my home-town, little knowing that the murky politics of a contested land would once again rip apart my assiduously restructured life. I also knew that Sonny had been living there with his wife and children since the declaration of general amnesty, but I came nonetheless, convinced that I was 'cured' of Sonny.

After two weeks with family and friends, when I was beginning to relax for the first time in many years, all hell broke loose and my world turned upside down once again. It all started with an early morning call from my niece who sobbed out the terrible news, 'Aunty, Sonny was assassinated last night in his home, they say by the J group.' I held on to the phone for a while but without saying a word put it down. Sonny, the man who dared the fates and tamed his passion to follow a dream, gunned down in cold blood; Sonny who had once told me, 'Sweetheart, you don't understand, this is something bigger than you or me and everything else put together.

88

This is my destiny.' Was this then the end of that colossal dream? Was it his destiny to die at the hands of fellow dreamers?

I sat on the unmade bed, not daring to move or do anything lest I break into tiny shards, so taut was I with my unutterable grief. My mother burst into the room but when she saw my face she knew I'd heard and quietly withdrew, almost on tiptoe. I continued my private wake in the semi-darkness of the room, the undrawn curtains obstructing the sunlight of an otherwise bright and sunny day of summer. But the darkness within my heart only deepened with each passing moment.

'Sonny dead' was something incomprehensible; what I had cherished and kept alive in my innermost being was the image of 'Sonny alive', the way I had remembered him all these years: vibrant and so full of hope. If it had been difficult to live a desolate life without him then, now I felt truly bereaved, more than ever before, though he had been out of my life these last twelve years. As I sat immobile on the bed, my mind went back to the period when the spectre of his final commitment to the 'cause', as he called it, loomed large like a dark cloud between us, though I never voiced my misgivings. Only when I realized that he was bent on a course that was leading him irrevocably away from my life, I told him, 'As long as I know that you are alive and well, I shall try to live with your absence.' He understood what I meant and after he vanished into his dream-world I received word through various channels, information about his personal well-being. Then after about two years, the messages became vague and far between. Sometimes only torn pieces of newspapers appeared with circled letters of the alphabet carrying some message. Many a time it would be so garbled that I could not make anything out of it. But even this tenuous thread of connection between us snapped in the fifth year, plunging me into an abyss of anger, bitterness and resentment against the man who had come into my life in the prime of my youth and uprooted me from my conventional moorings, carrying me to heights of love and passion I had never thought existed, only to leave me marooned on a stark landscape, all for an illusive dream.

As I sat on the bed and mourned the passing away of the man who had continued to be such a vital presence in my spirit, I recalled our last night together. By that time I knew that Sonny had finally committed himself and was going to China with a batch of recruits for training and acquiring much-needed arms from across the border. Neither of us uttered the dreaded word. But 'China' now stood between us, like an impassable ridge of ice blinding my vision with its brilliance and enormity and numbing my senses with its inevitability. It threatened to eclipse the deep love we had shared for the last three years. This night, we both knew, was going to hold the last precious moments of our enchanted life and neither of us wanted it to be marred in any way. When the new day dawned, we would be in different worlds and our lives would never be the same again.

A kind of unfamiliar restraint crept into our behaviour that surreal night as though we were enacting a formal farewell. Our bodies' responses remained as ardent and intense as before but we experienced a fierce desperation in our coming together as though we were fending off an unseen force that was tearing us away from each other. When passion was done, we were gripped by the unspoken terror of the truth floating in the silence. Wordlessly we clung to, and lay in each other's arms, but unlike other nights when such moments only replenished our need for each other, this night we were lost in the maze of thinking 'China'; I, resenting it, and he, never acknowledging nor apologizing for it though he must have sensed my fears in the urgency and ferocity of my response to his tender lovemaking.

The memory of that night reminded me of the way I had sneaked out of his life as though I were trying to prove that it was *I* and not he who was leaving the other. As the first light of dawn appeared on the horizon, I got up quietly, making sure that I did not disturb the gently snoring figure who was about to embark on a journey away from me, I went out for a long walk in the woods beyond the campus, creating a physical distance as a buffer against the impending abandonment, and stayed there until I felt sure that he had left for his ordained destination. When I came back to the cottage, it was filled with his absence and I felt as though it too, was dead just as I felt at that moment. A void settled in my heart as vast as the wide expanse of the woods I had just left out there. Absentmindedly I noticed that he had drunk the coffee I had left for him in the thermos. There was also a short note on the dresser which simply said, 'Sweetheart, this is not goodbye because you will forever be the love of my life.' In bitterness and frustration I tore it to pieces.

What neither of us had understood at that time was that Sonny was entering a twilight zone in the struggle for freedom where one could not identify the real enemy any more because the conflict was no longer only of armed resistance against an identifiable adversary. It had now also become an ideological battlefield within the resistance movement itself, posing new dangers from fellow national workers supposedly pursuing a common goal. And today Sonny had become a victim of his own convictions when the assassins pumped bullets into a fellow fighter's bosom.

Though Sonny had become a hero and intellectual 'guru' to the younger generation of sympathizers, he had a tendency to alienate the senior leaders of the movement by questioning their ideology and actions in public even before he went 'underground'. During those years when the world was avidly following the careers of a revolutionary called Fidel Castro and his friend and adviser Che Guevara, some of his admirers went to the extent of comparing Sonny to the enigmatic Che, claiming that he was the real brain of the entire movement. This certainly did not endear him to the powers within the movement and from the moment he joined their ranks, he had to walk a tight-rope in the multi-headed ideological minefield within.

When he quietly slipped away from my life into another sphere of existence, I was plunged into an abyss of self-doubt and self-recrimination for my obsessive love for a man who regarded his own nationalistic passion more important than the love of a woman. After a while though, I resolved that I, too, would seek a new environment where my work would help me to bear the pain of his absence from my life. So I moved to a big city where, after many months of hardship, I got a job with a national paper and began my career as a journalist. It turned out to be a strategic position as far as links with Sonny were concerned because stray bits of information about factional tensions within the various groups due to ideological differences would surface in journalistic circles now and then, which eventually reached my desk at the bureau. I often wondered how Sonny was dealing with the situation. Ever the impulsive and outspoken man that he was, I feared that sooner or later, he would say or do something to bring down the wrath of the bigger groups on himself or his family. But of one thing I was sure: Sonny would stand by his principles, come what may.

In the seventh year of my life 'after Sonny', a fellow reporter showed me a clipping from a foreign newspaper announcing the marriage of a 'rebel' leader with one of the female cadres in his outfit; I thought to myself, it could be any one of the so-called leaders. But the next sentence stunned me: it said that this particular leader had abandoned the prospects of a bright future as a constitutional lawyer to join the movement. And I knew that it could not be anyone else other than Sonny! If I ever really hated the man I had loved so much, it was at this moment. So enamoured was I with the idea of Sonny being as faithful to me as I was to him, that it had not occurred to me that he was now living in a totally different environment filled with the daily hazards of living in primitive conditions, and at the same time coping with danger from the superior forces of the government as well as threats from rival groups.

As I look back on that stage of my life I realize how extremely naive I was. I had often argued with him that he was living in a dream ignoring the realities of the world. I had even at times ridiculed his goal of achieving an independent state, asking him where his treasury or his army was. He would simply give me a cryptic smile, wink slyly and point to his head and say, 'Here'. If he was a dreamer then I too was one because I was still so immersed in the romantic haze of my first love that I completely failed to comprehend the new realities of his life away from mine. And the devastating news reminded me how far removed Sonny's world was from mine, and how changed he must have become with the compulsions of a totally new milieu. But no amount of rationalization could blunt my acute sense of feeling betrayed.

It was then that the façade of normalcy and conformity began to crack and I lost my way. I took up with men at the slightest encouragement and spent two stormy years of numerous flings. News of my profligacy reached home and my elder brother came to take me back to 'dry out' as he put it. There was a ragged bundle of letters at home among which were three from Sonny written two years earlier. I was stunned when I read them. In the first one he wrote about life on the run and the hardships faced by the group. The second one was pathetic: almost incoherent, it spoke of his disillusionment, frustration and suicidal tendencies due to not succeeding in his endeavours. And then an uncharacteristic confession: he wrote one sentence which still rings in my ears: 'Sweetheart, there were often times when I felt grateful that you did not try to stop me from going in, but now I wish you had.' This was a different Sonny from the one I knew and cherished: in a way it was a kind of disillusionment for me too; the man whom I had thought so strong and even infallible was human after all!

I did not open the last one for two days dreading its contents but curiosity got the better of me and I slit open the dirty envelope. It was short; it simply said 'No matter what you hear or read, know that my love for you is the one abiding truth of my life.' It was then that I knew that he was indirectly referring to his impending marriage. When we were together I used to be the one to speak of love; he could never bring himself to express sentimental feelings. But now he was speaking of his love for me virtually on the eve of his marriage, and I realized the sad truth that his actions were now determined by existential compulsions rather than personal feelings.

Linking the memory of those words to the present grief, I finally wept the inconsolable lament of the truly bereaved and cried until there were no more tears to shed for the man I had lost twice, once to his idealism and now to death. I recalled how, during those desert years of loneliness and aching, I had longed to have one more glimpse of that handsome face which had enthralled me, to hear the voice that seemed to caress me every time he uttered my name, and to be gathered in the embrace of the powerful yet gentle arms. I had felt so loved and sheltered then. And now all that was gone, and very soon the man called Sonny would become, if at all, a mere mention in some obscure history book.

As I sat on the bed and tried to absorb the fact of Sonny's death, my mind strayed to incongruous musings: what had happened to the bluish mole over his right nipple? Was it still intact or had the bullets obliterated it? How does the handsome face look in death? They must have dressed him in a suit by now, I thought, as I looked at the wall clock and saw that it was half past seven and again my mind went on to trivial details. What kind of shirt have they put on his shattered chest? Did his wardrobe still contain the blue silk tie I gave him for the Christmas of our last year together? I even began to smile, remembering the boyish pleasure he had evinced when he saw my present. That Christmas morning in the university chapel, when he turned up in a dark navy blue suit with a pale blue shirt and wearing the tie I had given him, my heart swelled with joy and pride: I thought no man on earth could look more handsome than Sonny and I gloried in the fact that he was mine!

The morning was no longer quiet; sounds of daily routine intruded, reminding me of where I was and what had happened. Earlier, one of my old friends from school had called. I took the call the third time on mother's insistence. She wanted to know if I would attend the funeral the next day and if I needed her with me. I muttered a curt 'no' and put the phone down. The funeral! But who would be buried? I still could not comprehend the finality of the word because in my mind Sonny would always be alive. But a funeral would be held; what would they bury with the ravaged remains of the man who once was the people's hope for a new life? The many funerary gifts of native shawls of course, also a few of his favourite possessions. And his ideology, would it be buried with his remains? I could no longer think coherently, and gradually a strange fusion of 'Sonny alive' and 'Sonny dead' began to take hold of my thinking, because I realized that only in death now, had he become more real to me than ever before.

When I embarked on the journey home, I believed that I had finally overcome the 'Sonny phase' of my life and that I had emerged a totally new person from that 'ordeal' by love. But his death had demolished that façade and exposed the truth of my love. Sonny had written that his love for me was the one abiding truth of his life and now I tearfully acknowledged that the same was true of my love for him. I had never really accepted his absence from my life as final; but his death, this horrible death finally obliterated all hope of ever seeing him again. Was that secret hope part of the reason which brought me to my parents' home?

As the morning wore on, a distant cousin who had lived with us since my school days came to my room asking me if I wanted some breakfast. When I shook my head she grinned! With the grin still on her face she said something strange, 'You should be glad that you did not marry Sonny.' I was so taken aback that I simply stared at her but when she turned to leave the room I threw the heavy brush with which I was fiddling at her retreating back, shouting 'Get out!' The brush landed on her head and she went out screaming for my mother. The crude remark of this feather-brained woman took me back to the period when Sonny and I were contemplating marriage after our studies were completed. But those were also the exciting days of national fervour that caught the imagination of all and sundry both in the rural and urban populace. For the so-called educated elite of the towns, the success of the movement meant setting up an independent country where the inequalities and injustices of the repressive 'occupation' forces would be eliminated. Not only that, but many lent their support with an eye to personal gains in the new set-up. But for the rural people, it was simply seen as an opportunity to return to the utopian state of self-rule before the alien rulers had come and overturned their ancient way of life.

The call to armed rebellion was like heady wine at first. But the retaliatory measures of the government forces blazed through the land like a wild fire, turning villages into burnt-out heaps, and people into creatures herded into concentration-camp-like grouping zones. Families were separated, women were raped and killed, and the men were forced to see the humiliation before they too, were either maimed for life or simply killed. These stories filtering through the urban grapevine only added fuel to the anger and hostility brewing in the minds of those pursuing higher education in various institutions in different cities. It was this turn of events that overshadowed our talk of marriage and I saw the gradual withdrawal of Sonny into a world quite estranged from our idyllic cohabitation. Compared to the fire that burned in his soul at that particular point of time, marriage must have seemed too trivial a matter to be contemplated.

My troubled reminiscences were however rudely interrupted when the cousin brought the morning papers. Sonny's face dominated all the front pages. I could not bear to look at the handsome face of Sonny so recently dead; so, folding the paper to hide it, I hurriedly glanced at the text. They all said more or less the same things. But one reporter had gone a step further: he reported that a former 'friend' of the slain leader was also in town and he wondered if she could throw more light on the reasons for this assassination! A 'friend' of Sonny in public parlance, but I know that I was once branded a 'fallen woman' because I was living 'in sin' with him. I knew exactly what he was aiming at: the kind of sensationalism that is created out of innuendos and vague remarks, tricks that as a journalist I too, had employed to make a story 'juicier'. This was however a new element which threatened to embroil me in an untenable situation because of my association with Sonny more than a decade ago.

Though I had not for a moment thought of attending the funeral, the remarks in the paper crystallized my decision. It seemed to clear my thinking. First of all, I said to myself, I cannot display the deep sorrow I felt at Sonny's death. So I took a leisurely bath, wore a bright dress and appeared at the dining table for lunch. Mother averted her eyes, father simply nodded, acknowledging my presence but the cousin gawked at me and was about to say something when the front door opened and my brother and his wife walked in. If they were surprised to see me so calm and composed, they did their best not to show it. The meal went off well, with mother taking care to send the feckless cousin on an errand to a neighbour's house. Some visitors came, among them my friends from university days. The atmosphere was strained but I remained calm throughout. Somehow the afternoon wore off and by about five the family was left alone.

Mother called my sister-in-law to the kitchen, and my brother said, 'Let's go out for a walk.' I was surprised, because after my 'flirtatious binge' some years ago my puritanical brother always treated me as a 'cured' leper. But sensing that he had something important to say, I followed him outside. When we were out of sight from the house, he produced a thick envelope and handed it to me without saying anything. I did not accept it immediately but asked, 'What is this?' He looked at me steadily for a long time during which I could almost see his face change from his earlier aversion to something bordering on understanding. He came closer and embracing me, said in a broken voice, 'I should have given it to you much earlier; please forgive me if you can.' He walked away abruptly without a backward glance. Hugging the envelope I continued to walk for some more time and came home as dusk was enveloping everything around.

I went straight to my room and bolting the door, tore open the mysterious packet. For the second time that day I felt that I was hit by lightning; inside the envelope was a floppy and a short note from Sonny dated, it seemed, centuries ago. I was stunned and it took me some time to open the letter and read the message from the dead; it spoke of his anguish over a host of things, among which he said the heaviest burden was his feeling of guilt towards me. But the main issue was the floppy which, he wrote, was his testament about the true state of the movement and he wanted me to publish it by any means. I was somewhat disappointed and wished he had written a longer letter telling me how much he still loved and missed me. But his words were terse as always and I detected a note of urgency in the tone. I had to be content with his last lines which said, 'Sweetheart, forgive me for burdening you with this dangerous task, but you are the only one I can trust.' And he signed off 'Yours always and forever, Sonny.' No words about love or longing, only the vague 'forever' which I hugged to myself, and I began to cry again.

My inner grief having been spent, I began to fling the most essential things into an overnight bag because I decided to leave immediately, without even telling my family. I tried several hiding places for the letter and the floppy, the secret compartment at the bottom of the bag, a roll of toilet paper, but gave up each idea. In the meantime I took out my return ticket which was still valid. But the airport was three hours' journey from my home. How was I going to reach it on time unless I started very early in the morning? In desperation I started to thumb through my tattered phone book. In a corner under T, I came across the name of an old friend whom I had not seen for ages and who, I was told, had started a transport business. With all my hope pinned on the currency of his number, I called him. After a long time a child answered and told me papa was out, gone to the dead man's house. I waited for another hour and called again and this time 'papa' answered. I warned him not to take my name and said I needed his help to go to the airport the next morning. He was hesitant at first saying that he had to attend Sonny's funeral. But sensing the urgency in my voice, he reluctantly agreed to arrange a taxi and asked me to be at the second corner from my house at four in the morning. And as an afterthought he asked me if anyone knew about my journey; when I said 'Not yet', he said 'Good, keep it that way,' and disconnected.

I joined the family for dinner and tried to put up a nonchalant attitude all throughout. I even stayed back to chat with my parents inquiring about their health and other mundane things. After some time my father stood up saying he was tired and said we should all get a good night's rest. After he left, mother hugged me goodnight and said an uncanny thing, 'Whatever you do, I will always understand.' Her words ringing in my ears, I went to my room and once again began to devise a foolproof hiding place for Sonny's floppy. Finally I hid it inside a packet of sanitary napkins which went into my hand baggage. Next, the letter; I was determined to keep it safe because it was my last link with Sonny. I tucked it carefully into my brassiere as I'd seen many women do with money. I was ready. But I could not leave without saying something to mother, so I wrote a brief note addressed to my parents; 'Dear Mom and Dad, please forgive me for sneaking away like this. But you know it's for the best.'

I did not sleep at all that night. The spectre of Sonny alive and Sonny dead haunted me with grief, frustration, anger and remorse, so relentlessly that a few times I almost choked on my suppressed screams. It also amazed me that even after death Sonny was the force that was dictating my life, and the old hatred I had felt on hearing of his marriage seemed once again to overwhelm the enormous grief in my heart at his passing away. But these conflicting moments were temporary and what settled in my mind eventually was the void I had felt that day when he left me. If that void had somehow been made bearable by hope, this time around I knew it was there to haunt me all my life.

Before sunrise, I crept out of the house with my small bags and walked to the appointed place. The man was waiting; he had come only to say goodbye, he said, because it was imperative that he be seen at Sonny's funeral and so had arranged another driver for me. We could hardly see each other clearly but I knew instinctively that he too, was under some tension, which he was trying to hide from me. When it was time for me to go, he gave me a hug and whispered in my ear, 'No matter what Sonny asked you to do, for God's sake and ours, don't do it.' And with a breezy 'Take care' he got into his car and drove off. It was only after I was on my way that his words registered: how did he know I had a missive from Sonny? My head began to spin with the realization that we were all enmeshed in this terrible thing, some of us through such insidious ways that it was impossible to determine any more who was what. And there was mother, an innocuous housewife, yet with such accurate perceptions about my anxiety! Was it only a woman's intuition or was some other network in operation? But most baffling was the behaviour of the taxi owner who had been a close confidant of Sonny and had been 'interrogated' by the security forces several times. But each time he had been let off, and it was rumoured that his recent business success was due to a generous 'loan' from the government.

And the most amazing thing of all was that he had not once mentioned Sonny's death, only the public funeral! Why, I asked myself. The more I pondered over these facts, the more convinced I became that Sonny's assassination was a well-calculated 'hit' of the underground power brokers and that somehow this quiet business man was a vital link in the puzzle. I also realized that I would never be totally free of this sinister web which had claimed Sonny's life because of the legacy he had left me. I could have simply destroyed it but I went to my bank and hired a safe deposit box, ostensibly to keep some jewellery that my mother had given me. I cannot explain why I did that because I did not even try to find out what the floppy contained. Only the letter, I keep next to my heart.

So the unread testament will lie there in its hiding place. When it is reclaimed by my inheritors, they will uncover, at the bottom of the box filled with junk jewellery, a mouldy, outdated floppy which no machine would ever be able decipher. It is better that way. I am no longer affected by news from home about the political aftermath of Sonny's assassination; but the brutality of his death still sears my heart as if the bullets had struck me too. And when I heard that Sonny's close confidant quietly went underground and became the new leader of Sonny's band of 'freedom fighters', I understood why Sonny had written that he could trust only me. Was it because I was apolitical? Or was he so confident of my love for him that even after so many years and so many barriers between us he believed that I would still do his bidding? I shall never know. In the meantime the convoluted politics of the ravaged land continue in the self-diminishing moves and counter moves of a people living in limbo. And I? I live on with the debris of a passionate carnival because I had once loved a dream-chaser named Sonny.

Flight

Life began for me in the wide open spaces of a vast cabbage field, in fact, on the underside of a big leaf near the passage-ways between the rows of plants, which criss-crossed the entire length and breadth of the field. From the minuscule speck of a seed left by the flitting mother, I slowly evolved into an elongated green form, blending in perfectly with the big leaf.

One bright, sunny morning, there was a piercing shriek, heard along the length and breadth of the field, 'Eek, a caterpillar, a caterpillar!' Then murmurs of many different voices; the woman continued her shrieking. Was it fear I heard in that voice, or was it disgust? I was not sure. Then, a little girl's voice, 'Ugh! It's so ugly.'

Another voice intruded, 'Wow, look at him, isn't he beautiful? Mother, can I keep him? Please—I'll put him in a shoebox in my room, he won't disturb anybody, I promise. And he will be my dragon.' Silence all around, as though everyone was holding their breath. I was beginning to panic; maybe this was going to be my last day.

Then a man's voice, all choked with emotion, 'Yes Johnny, you may keep him. Put your dragon-box on the dresser beside your bed. And remember, you will be responsible for any consequence regarding this.'

'Hurray! Thanks Father,' the boy shouted. Someone snipped the leaf from the base of the cabbage and handed it to the boy.

He held it gingerly. As Johnny entered his bedroom and proceeded to prepare this strange space for my new life I felt as though I was being transported to another world.

Sounds of things being scattered, more rummaging and doors being slammed. Finally, the little boy exclaimed, 'Ah, here it is.' I wondered what he had found as he gingerly put me on a soft surface. As I continued wondering, strange activities were taking place, papers being torn and cut. 'H'm, this will do,' Johnny muttered to himself at last.

Suddenly I was being lifted and lowered into some dark place. I looked up; Johnny was gazing at me with a strange smile on his face, 'Go to sleep, dragon, I'll see you in the morning.' And total darkness, as he shut the lid.

At that instant, my former life of wide-open spaces and bright sunshine vanished, and the new one of intermittent light and darkness began. Light, when he opened the lid to peep at me, and then darkness again when he lowered it. The periods between light and darkness were regular to begin with, but as time went on, they became longer and longer. Sometimes days would go by without a glimpse of light.

Then one evening, I heard footsteps approaching the bedroom where Johnny was sleeping. These days, he slept most of the time, day or night. I was beginning to think that he had lost interest in me. The footsteps entered the room; I heard the swish of a woman's dress, silk perhaps, and oh! the faintest whiff of something strange I'd never smelled before. The parents were talking in whispers, and then the father opened the lid of the box and I saw a row of brilliant stars around the woman's neck. The man said, 'Look at his dragon,' and the woman stifled a heart-rending sob. 'Hush,' the man said, 'you must be strong. He does not feel the pain now.' The lid was dropped shut and once again darkness enveloped me as the footsteps receded into the night.

Time became a blur for me. Strange sensations were taking place in my body. I felt bogged down by some alien weight and was no longer the same being that Johnny had so lovingly kept as his captive dragon in the darkness of the limited space. I began to feel restless and longed for the open spaces of my earlier life.

In the midst of all this confusion within me, one day, there was a big commotion in the house. People running about and shouting, 'Hurry up—careful, mind the steps,' and in the midst of all this, Johnny's feeble voice, 'I want my dragon, I want my dragon.' With a jerk, my universe of darkness was lifted by rough, impatient hands and the next thing I knew, I was in a stranger place, a room reeking of some very strong smells. I heard children crying and even grown-up voices whimpering with pain and sadness. I do not know how long we were there, I only know that Johnny was there too, because his breathing was becoming hoarser by the day. Each time his parents came into the room, the whispers of the other place were now replaced by anguished sobs.

Then one afternoon, there was an unearthly sound, one resonating with wild fear, from the mother, because the rattling sound was gone from Johnny's breath. The echo of that sound shivered through me and I thought that something terrible had happened to him. But then a new calm returned as the old rattle in Johnny's throat started again. After a little while, I heard Johnny's feeble voice saying, 'I want to see my dragon.'

Gently, the sister opened the lid and exclaimed, 'Look, a butterfly, how beautiful it is!' Johnny strained to peer closer, gazed at me in disgust and disbelief, and countered, 'Beautiful? Dragon, what happened to you? You look ugly.' So saying, he slumped back and remained still.

Gingerly, I flapped my new-grown wings, took a tentative step on new-found legs and with a flourish came out of my dark prison. I perched on the window sill and looked around. Oh! It was bright and airy out there, beyond the place where Johnny lay amidst rumpled clothes, the rattle in his throat sounding harsh in the stillness as everyone seemed rooted to the floor. Johnny's sister made as if to catch me but I quickly shifted to a higher ledge. At that instant I knew that I was ready to venture out into the space away from the reach of Johnny's world.

As I fluttered my wings for the final take-off, a tiny voice within me said, 'Wait, what about Johnny? Are you going to leave him all alone?' I hesitated for the briefest while, but I knew I had to leave his dying universe. I looked at his pale, grief-stricken face but my resolve was stronger than the appeal in his eyes. As though propelled by an unknown force, I flapped my wings and was soon fleeting away without a backward glance, the worm within me urging, 'Fly, you are your own universe now, fly to your destiny.'